Jason's Promise

No choice, no option, no other way

Roy Swanberg

Sterling Rock
Books

7/7/14

Ron,

Thanks for the second cup of coffee and the encouragement.

Roy Swanberg

Heb 10:23

JASON'S PROMISE
No choice, no option, no other way

Published by
Sterling Rock Books
576 Boyd Ave.
Princeton
IL 61356
United States of America

Dedication

To Michelle and Kristin
Two young ladies
I'm proud to call daughters

This is the first of a three book, character driven, series.

Book Two: *Jason's Promise, Put to the Test.*
Jason meets the moral and ethical challenges of college life and law school.

Book Three: *Jason's Promise, Fulfilled.*
The story of Jason in the roughness of the political arena.

Chapter One

Thirteen-year-old Jason Greene's eyelids snapped open like runaway window shades. He had been waiting for this day a long time. He untangled his lanky frame from twisted sheets, showered, dressed, and jumped down the stairs four at a time like he had been told not to do for years.

Landing in the kitchen he slid over the hardwood flooring in his white socks and opened the silverware drawer and cabinets like a possessed man. With one hand he shoveled cereal into his face, calling that breakfast, and with a knife loaded with peanut butter he crafted a peanut butter and jelly sandwich on two slabs of bread for his lunch.

Michelle, his mother, leaned against the counter, arms folded across her chest, shaking her head in a silent No, betraying the fact she knew something Jason didn't.

"You look excited today, son. Where you off to?"

"Bike ride, Mom. Remember, yesterday I told you the guys and me were going to ride out to the new Captain Swift covered bridge and have lunch by the river."

Without moving a muscle, "You didn't tell me yesterday. When I got home from work you had your head stuck in that silly movie about the two dumb guys – for the third time this week."

"Oh yeah, I forgot. Chris, Tim, and Shawn …"

"Hold on, favorite one. There seems to be a breakdown in communication here."

"Whadda mean, Mom?"

"Number one, you *didn't* tell me. Number two, there's some tall grass in the yard calling your name for the third day in a row. You promised your dad you'd have the yard looking sharp when he got home from National Guard Camp." Holding up two fingers, "Two days, son."

Disappointed and angry with himself, he dropped the knife on the floor where it stuck without a bounce. He slouched onto a nearby stool and pleaded, "Mom, Mom, I can do the yard tomorrow. We gotta do the ride today."

"I hear what you're saying and I feel the pain to come, but you *did* promise your dad the yard would take one of his inspections when he got home. Rain is coming tomorrow."

"What am I gonna tell the guys, Mom?"

"You and your dad have been hitting this responsibility bit pretty hard lately, and it's about to come back and bite you today."

"Messed up big time, didn't I!" Jason shook his head in defeat while handing his mother the sandwich. "Want a peanut butter and jelly sandwich?"

"You amaze me more and more. You came off your high pretty well this time. Just before he left for camp, your dad said he thought you were growing up."

"Well, Mom, maybe I am. I jus—" The ringing of the doorbell cut him off.

Sprinting toward the door, Jason called back, "I'll get it. I'm sure it's the guys."

The words, "Yard first," followed him from the kitchen.

"Yeah, yeah, yeah. Yard first," Jason muttered under his breath as he opened the door.

Expecting to see his friends, he was stunned to be looking into the broad chests of an army major and a lieutenant colonel chaplain. Rev. Larsen, his own minister, was with them.

"Awfully quiet in there. Who is it, Jay?" Michelle's voice came from the kitchen.

In a high pitched squeaking whisper, hanging in the air, "Cm'ere, Mom."

When Michelle came into the living room and saw the men, she stopped quickly, brought her hands to her face, and being a military wife, read the scene in an instant.

"Jason, come here," she said.

She grabbed the boy and held him tight as Rev. Larsen reached out and held them both in an unspoken painful embrace that left nothing to be said.

Jason's empty and hollow eyes flashed for answers. "Mom, Mom, does this mean what I think it does?"

The two officers stepped into the house, quietly closing the door without any further invitation,

Jason could see his mom's hand trembling as she searched for the arm of a chair. "Jason, sit here with me."

After a moment of awkward silence, Jason got up, and being used to seeing his father in a major's uniform, looked for his dad's face above the golden oak leafs of the man standing in front of him, but his dad's face refused to show.

Pastor Larsen was the first to speak. "Michelle, Jason, I'm so sorry to come here today. These officers have some hard news to tell you."

"Mrs. Greene ... Jason," the chaplain started, putting his hand on the boy's shoulder. "I too am sorry I have to stand here in your home. I have the awful job of telling you ..." He looked at Michelle. "Last night your husband Marc," then looking right into Jason's flashing ebony eyes, "your father, lost his life in a training exercise at camp in Minnesota."

Jason felt his heart going into shock, freezing like a block of ice and sinking into his stomach with cutting speed. In a numb stupor he stepped behind his mother and put his arms around her neck.

"Son, do you understand this?"

Leaning over and burying his face in her hair. "Mom, I know just what it means." His voice cracking over the words. "Dad's not coming back." Quickly standing, he asked, "How did it happen, Major?"

"Your father died in a helicopter crash, with four others, during a training maneuver. It looks as if there was a mechanical problem that took the chopper down. There is an investigation going on right now."

If Jason ever had the urge to run, it was now. He did.

Bolting through the kitchen, still in his white socks, he didn't even slow down as he pushed the screen door open so hard it swung back and slammed into the siding. With blurry eyes, and lungs so seared with grief he could hardly breathe, he ran to the big post by the steps. This was *his* post. It had markings on it showing his growth since the day he could stand up at eight months. He tightly wrapped his arms around the post as if it was the only solid thing in his life right now. He needed it for support – he could feel himself growing faint and weak.

He squeezed the post and looked around the yard. All he could see were reminders of his dad. The swing set they put up together when he was four, by now long unused and only an obstacle to mowing. They had plans to take it down when his dad returned from camp. The tree house in the big oak he and his dad would occasionally sleep in, and that long grass that now burned his heart with guilt and shame.

Jason blinked his slippery eyes at the post and saw the most recent entry his dad made the day he left for camp, just ten days ago. *My son is becoming a man.* He recalled joking with his dad about being a man. He twisted his forehead on the message, deliberately ignoring John Carlson, his neighbor he could see washing his car in the shared driveway cul-de-sac extension.

Chapter Two

Jason looked into the garage and spotted his bike lying on its side, right where he left it yesterday. If running out of the house helped a few minutes ago, a good strong bike ride around town would clear his head. He quickly put on some ratty old shoes that were on the porch, ran to the bike, grabbing the handlebars with both angry and hurt emotions so hard that the wheels left the floor and bounced on the tires.

Without seeing clearly, he stood hard on the pedals and shot out the open garage door like a runaway horse, forgetting John Carlson washing his new Escalade in the driveway. He smashed dead on into the grillwork of the car so hard he flew off the bike, rolled up over the hood, and dropped off the right side of the car into a heap on the wet concrete. He became aware of John running to see if he was okay; and as his neighbor started to help him up he went ballistic.

Jason squirmed and flayed his arms. *"Don't touch me! Leave me alone! Leave me alone!"*

"Jason, what's wrong? This isn't like you."

Jason felt John's arms lifting him up, and with confused emotions and growing fear he began to strike out at his neighbor.

"Jay, Jay, Jay! You don't know your own strength. You're pounding on me like an eighteen year old."

He heard John's words, yet they did not stop him from stiffening his body, twisting and kicking in his efforts to be free. Then he felt John's strength increase around him. It stopped him from doing more damage to himself or the car.

"Jay, what is it? What's wrong?" John demanded.

Spitting back words filled with anger and fear, Jason yelled, *"You don't know what's going on! You wouldn't care! No one cares!"*

Jason could feel John squeezing his head with his hands, but he kept twisting away. Then he was aware of John putting his face close to his.

"Jason, Jason! It's me, John. Now what is it? Tell me."

"Dad was killed at camp last night. Some army chaplain is in the house with Mom and Pastor Larsen."

At the words of such heartbreak, John crushed Jason's head to his chest. "Oh, dear Lord. Let it go, Jay. Fight, scream, cry. Let it all out, my friend."

In another attempt to free himself from John's grip, Jason flung his hands and arms back and forth, tearing the collar and pocket off John's old shirt. After popping buttons on the driveway, he finally fell limp, weak and exhausted in John's arms. "I can't go back there right now. Don't make me – please!"

Jason loosed his grip on his neighbor, and felt him doing the same. He stood looking down at the driveway, then realized John, with tears in his own eyes, was looking up at where Rev. Larsen was standing with his hand on Jason's special post as though not wanting to interrupt.

"Why are you crying, Mr. Carlson? It was *my* dad that died, not yours."

"Jay, you know your dad was like an older brother to me. This hurts me too. What's more, I'm holding his son like he would want to. You've just been hit with the worst news you'll ever hear in your life. You're too young to go through this."

"Aw gee, Mr. Carlson, look, I wet my pants."

"Don't let it bother you. We'll blame it on the wet driveway where you fell."

From inside her kitchen, Karen, John Carlson's wife, saw what was going on in the driveway, but didn't know why Jason acted so tormented. Wiping her hands on a towel as she came down the steps she saw her neighbor Michelle Greene, the two officers and Rev. Larsen coming from the other house. John told Karen the news and she instinctively reached to her young neighbor and hugged him – wet clothes and all. She then reached out to Michelle with an embrace only a close neighbor could offer at this point.

"I'm sorry I ran out on you, Mom," Jason said as he went to his mother. "I just couldn't stand to be in there. Oh, um, I got all wet when I fell off my bike."

"That's the least of our problems now, son."

"Yeah, I guess so."

The officers finished their condolences and promised Michelle they would do all they could to help with the service arrangements.

Rev. Larsen said, "Michelle, I'll stay with you and Jason until your sister Denise and her husband Rob can get here from Ravenswood. About an hour away, isn't it?"

Michelle nodded yes.

When Jason went in to change clothes, John Carlson picked up the bike and put it in his garage to fix later.

His wife, Karen, helped him finish washing the car.

"Boy, Jason sure finished off your old pullover shirt."

"You know, for some strange reason just last week, Jason told me he wanted to have this old thing when I got done with it."

Karen, frowned. "Why would he —"

"I have no idea."

"It was deep purple the day I gave it to you when we were engaged ten years ago. You looked great in it then. Now you look like a pink hulk in it."

"Guess it shrunk, huh?"

"John, how can you be funny at a time like this?"

"We'd better finish things up here and change into better clothes. This neighborhood is going to get crowded real soon."

"Oh, John, I feel so sorry for Michelle and Jason. They're just like family to us aren't they?"

John nodded his head with tightly closed eyes and set jaws.

Rev. Larsen's wife and another couple from church arrived shortly, and again the tears flowed freely while hugs cushioned grieving hearts.

In an hour, Denise and her husband Rob arrived. The hurt and pain, like blood spurting from a torn artery, flowed again. For the rest of the day friends started to come by and the phone rang constantly.

"Uncle Rob, why do all these people have to come over now? Jason asked.

"In a town like this, news travels fast, Jay. Lots of people knew your dad, and they all feel they have to say or do something for you and your mom. Be kind to them, and thank them for their thoughts. Every one of them will be truly sorry."

The bike ride and mow the yard argument were quickly forgotten as the house filled with people. Two neighbors from across the street brought their lawn mowers over and mowed Jason's neglected yard. Jason again went to the back porch and hugged his post where he could be alone with his thoughts.

"Dad, Dad," he whispered, "what will my life be like without you? We were just getting to be good friends since the canoe trip. Dad, please drive up the driveway – now."

He looked into the blue sky spotted by white clouds. Memories of the canoe trip a year ago with his dad began playing in his searching, confused, and shredded mind like a movie on a DVD.

Chapter Three

Earlier in the spring, a year ago, Jason remembered how he had balked at a five-day trip with just his dad, thinking how it sounded dorkey. Besides, he was twelve years old, and he and his friends had made lots of plans for the summer. After some creative nudging from his dad, videos of John Carlson's own canoe trips, and a promise that John would personally fly them up to Duluth in a rented plane, Jason got his head fully into the trip. August couldn't come fast enough.

As the plane approached the hills of Duluth, Jason, with his face pressed to the window in his first flight, started to unroll questions that wouldn't stop for a week.

"How long is it going to take to paddle a canoe across that lake?"

"That's Lake Superior," Jason's dad, Marc, said with a snicker, while John Carlson, neighbor and pilot, laughed out loud. "We're not going to cross that one. We have many more miles by truck before we get to the lakes we're going to be in

"Wow, I'm glad to hear that. That's why they call it a great lake, huh?"

"There ya go, son."

Upon landing they were met by Moose, a tall and solid college kid in a red and black checkered flannel shirt hanging out over a twisted belt that was struggling to hold up his baggy pants. Jason guessed the man with the unkempt beard was twentyish, and well deserving of the name. Moose said he was an employee of Cherokee Outfitters, and introduced Marc and Jason to his old beat-up bright neon orange pickup with BIG ORANGE painted boldly on the sides of the hood, and a smirk of a smile across the grillwork. The number five was crossed out and six painted above the grill.

"What's the six for?" Jason asked.

"That's the number of deer I've gotten with this truck; fully dead on contact. Bouncing deer off the fenders and near misses don't count."

"Wow!" Jason yelled, "I like that, and the color. Why such a bright orange?"

"In hunting season that orange stops bullets from coming my way."

They threw their gear in the bed of the truck and drove north about ninety-eight miles up the breathtaking North Shore to Tofte, Minnesota.

Along the way, Jason said repeatedly, "This trip is awesome, nothing like Illinois." To his left he saw tall granite rocky cliffs with water tumbling over them, and to the right Lake Superior. "Is that an ocean?" he blurted out, suddenly realizing that was impossible. Fortunately no one seemed to hear, or maybe they pretended not to. If so, he was glad.

Tofte, on the rocks facing Lake Superior, housed all of a post office, bar, and gas station/convenient mart. Moose said it was the perfect place for a stretch, to take on a last minute supply of junk food, and a potty break.

When Moose pulled away from the station, BIG

ORANGE threw up some Minnesota real-estate behind it. Jason yelled, "Cool."

A left turn off of state 61 took the three onto a twenty-two mile bumpy and dusty road that looked more like a trip through a canyon of fir trees, and ended up at their first lake in the Superior National Forest. At the Cherokee Outfitters lodge they rented a canoe and all the supplies, including food they would need for the odyssey to come.

When the canoe and gear were put together at the water's edge, Jason's questions rolled again.

"Where's the motor, Dad?"

"Too much TV," Marc joked as he picked up the two paddles, held them at arm's length, and said, "Son, behold, the motor."

Jason tilted his head and looked at his dad as if he had been slapped with one of the paddles. He noticed his dad grin as though thinking that this might be a long trip.

After the canoe was fully packed, bright orange life jackets on, and the gear wrapped neatly under plastic in the center, Jason asked. "Why do we have to wrap all this in plastic?"

"Something tells me you'll find out before the day is over. Jay, we're going to pray before we shove off."

Pray about a canoe? What was his dad getting at? But he noticed his dad did pray a lot in the past year. Not only did he pray a lot, but things were a lot better in their lives since his dad became a Christian: whatever that had to do with anything – or even a canoe trip.

"Okay, Dad," Jason said after the prayer. "You sit up front so you can show us where to go, and I'll sit in the back and be the power for this cruise ship."

"Jay, I think ... No, let's not argue. You'll learn faster that way."

Jason shrugged, and slipped into the stern seat while his dad shoved off from the bow, and the canoe drifted out to "sea." Jason juggled his paddle from one side to the other, splashing water like a drowning man, pounding dents into the aluminum and proving a quick answer as to why the plastic covering. He was about to say, "I quit," when he managed to have the canoe heading straight back to the pier where the bow chipped off a hunk of wood.

Out of the corner of his eye, Jason saw two fishermen and Moose standing nearby, obviously observing this sorry show of seamanship, smile at each other, roll their eyes back into their heads and laugh, before walking back up the hill.

With a few adjustments in crew assignments, they were off towards the north end of the lake. It only took a few minutes for Jason to start spilling questions again.

"Why isn't there anything out here, Dad? No roads, cars, or buildings. Nothing around here except water, trees, and sky. No telephone poles, wires, or people."

"That's it, Jay. A different world. Sort of like being on another planet."

"How do we get to the other lakes? Who takes care of the stuff?"

"You'll see."

"Where's the motel? Where do we eat?"

"You'll learn it all in the next few days."

Jason heard his dad whisper, "Lord, I love this kid."

"Is there a bathroom?"

His dad's quiet answer to question after question was a calm, "You'll see.. I want you to understand how little you know about life outside of Prairie Heights. Over the next five days you're going to discover this new world and the answers to your questions. This trip up Sawbill Lake and the other lakes on a canoe trip is something only a handful of young sons and their dads are privileged to take. I'm glad we can do it."

They paddled the canoe in silence for some time as Jason took in the amazing scenery and the almost overwhelming sense of isolation.

At last his dad spoke. "Son, I haven't told you before, but just a year ago John Carlson led me to the Lord."

Jason frowned and tilted his head. "I didn't think people *become* Christians. You were *born* one."

His dad glanced at him. "I guess you don't understand what I'm talking about, but I hope you've noticed that my life has changed because of Christ."

Jason kept silent. Puzzled. Yes, his dad had changed in many ways. More peaceful. More like the dad he wanted.

"Jay, you're twelve now. Almost a teenager. That's why I want to do something special with you before too many changes come. I want you to do some heavy thinking on this trip. I want it to be something you'll remember for the rest of your life, and come to see that obstacles of all sorts can be overcome."

Again Jason stayed silent. But turning around on the canoe seat and letting his dad do all the paddling, he studied his father closely, seeing him not just as his dad, but as a thirty-five-year-old high school teacher who was in exceptionally good shape as a result of his advanced workout program, playing football in high school and college, and being a major in the Illinois National Guard.

It was hot now, and the heat of that August day encouraged his father to remove the life jacket, then his shirt, exposing heavy bronzed shoulders and well developed arms. He put the life jacket back on and Jason thought his dad looked kinda cool. He suddenly realized his dad was doing all the work to keep the canoe moving, and he could see that the effort of being the main source of power in this adventure was causing the sweat to glisten in the hot sun as it rolled off his dad's broad back.

Imitating his dad, Jason took off his own shirt and stuffed it under the seat in the bow of the little ship. His shoulders were soft, chest and arms yet simple of form and white as a ghost.

Jason noticed his dad watching him, and wondered what he was thinking.

His father laughed. "Don't worry, son, you're a chip off the old block. You'll have a body like this! Wait until we've finished this trip. You'll have a tan and muscles on you that you'll be proud to show your friends."

Upon arriving at the start of the first portage a reoccurring question surfaced again. "Dad, I gotta go to the bathroom, bad. Where's the bathroom?"

"See that tree over there? Water it."

"Really? Can I?"

"Lesson number one when roughing it, son."

Chapter Four

Standing in a clearing where they beached the canoe, his dad said, "This is also the answer to your question about getting to another lake."

Jason turned right around. "I don't see anything but trees. I didn't know there were so many trees in the world. What's that nice smell?"

"Pine, son, pine. We'll be living in it for the whole week."

"It's the same smell you can buy in a little green Christmas tree for your car, huh? Well, how do we get to the next lake?"

"See that path going through the trees? It's called a portage. It's our way to the next lake. We carry all the stuff and walk it, just like the voyageurs back in the day."

"You mean we gotta carry all this stuff – ourselves?"

"Look around. See anyone else? No choice, no option, no other way. Just do it."

They removed the plastic cover, backpacks full of food and clothes, sleeping bags, tent, camera, water jugs, and other things and transferred the heavy load from the canoe to their backs. Only the canoe and paddles were left.

"What about these, dad?"

"We'll come back for them."

"What if someone takes 'em?"

"Jay, have you seen another human body around here in the past three hours?"

"I guess it will be okay."

The wood sign at the entrance to the path read, "Ada Lake 78 rods."

"How long is a rod, Dad?"

"Sixteen and a half feet. Remember that when it comes up in school, and you'll be the smart one."

Seventy-eight rods were no walk in the park. Steep hills up and steeper hills down were muddied from recent rains. Jason saw tall dead trees leaning on other stronger green trees as he stepped over fallen tree trunks and rushing streams of water crossing the portage. Hundreds of tree roots entwined themselves on the path, and the native mosquitoes were dining on their first fresh meat in days.

Getting to the other end, Jason dropped to his knees and rolled over onto his backpack. "Boy, glad that's over."

"Stay here, son," his dad said as he took off his backpack. "I'll go back and get the canoe."

"No way." Jason said, wiggling free from his burdens. "I'm not staying here alone."

Arriving back at the canoe, everything was as they left it. Refreshed by now, Jason said, "Hey, Dad, I saw a guy on TV once carry a canoe on his shoulders. Let me do it. You get the paddles."

Jason saw his dad smiling with a *he'll learn* look as he grabbed the two paddles and started up the path, leaving Jason to struggle with seventy pounds of aluminum while making a weak bleat for help.

Still walking on up the trail and not looking back, his dad called out, "Just like tough lessons in life, ya just gotta suck it up and tough it out."

"I don't think I can, Dad."

"Sure you can. Put all the Jason you got into it."

After a little more hard labor, stumbling around and snapping off tree branches, Jason said in a quiet voice, just loud enough for his father to hear, "Okay, Dad, I learned another one, didn't I?"

Jason was relieved to see his dad smiling as he returned to the scene of carnage to give him a high five. Jason took the paddles, and his father stepped next to the center of the canoe, grabbed the gunwales, and in one massive move lifted it up over his head. Jason's eyes bugged out like a stepped-on toad and dropped his jaw.

I'm gonna do that some day, I really am, Jason promised himself. "Hey Dad, how do you know where to go when the canoe is over your head?"

"Just watch the path at your feet."

Even though he was only carrying the two paddles and a back pack, Jason lowered his head and tried watching just the path at his feet, hoping his dad didn't see him.

Soon they got all the gear back into the canoe and started paddling through Ada Lake. Jason could feel the canoe picking up speed and saw splashing water in front of them. Pointing at the rushing water and looking back at his dad in fear, Jason yelled, "What's that? How do we get through that?"

"That, my son, looks like white water. Rapids tumbling through rocks and shallow water. Hold on to your paddle and let me do the work."

Jason turned to watch his father spread his legs as much as he could to stabilize the canoe as it twisted its way through the water, lunging up and down and banging into the rocks. Jason tightened his jaws, held his breath in fear, and looked back at his savior many times.

"Gonna make it, Dad?" he yelled about every four seconds.

"We'll make it, Jay. Just do as I say. Stay in the center of the seat and hold on to the gunwales."

After what seemed to be hours fighting rapids and the possibility of an early death, they were floating softly in Skoop Lake.

Jason let out a long gasp. "Whew, that took a long time."

"Son, it was only fifteen minutes." his dad said, laughing.

"You're good. Where did you learn all that?"

"Oh, just something I picked up from an old Apache Indian chief."

"Come on, Dad, you never knew an old Apache Indian. Not a chief anyway. Besides, didn't they live in the far southwest where it's hot and dry all the time? They probably never knew what a canoe looked like. You were scared too, weren't you?"

"You're right, Jay, I don't know any chief, and I didn't know the rapids were coming. Yes, I was scared too."

"I'm glad you were back there. By the way, how do we go back up that stuff on our way back?"

"Good thinking. I guess there are only two ways. Walk right in the water, or portage around it in the thick forest. In fact, I'm going to let you make the decision when the time comes. Neither will be easy."

Before the day lost its light, they had crossed Skoop Lake, another lake, and made two more portages until they came to an established, yet vacant small campsite on a point jutting out into Frost Lake. Jason felt there was little muscle left in his body, and he just wanted to sit.

"Build a fire, boy," his dad ordered, sounding more like Major Greene on duty than a father. "Set up the tent, unpack the gear, fix dinner, and let's eat. I'm as hungry as that bear over there."

"*Bear? Where?*" Jason shrieked, as he shot straight up off the ground and spun in a complete three-sixty while his cap didn't move.

"Easy, son, just kidding. We probably won't see any bears around here. Let's do this stuff together and enjoy our first night of sleep."

"Sleep way out here? On the ground? No cabin? Just us? Alone?"

"Jason, dear son, you do know we're on a canoe trip, don't you? Why is this taking so long to sink in? Didn't the trip through the rapids show you we're in a new world?"

"I don't know. I'll figure it out."

"Please, and do it in a hurry."

The little village was soon in operation, and after dinner, exhausted, they doused the campfire before crawling into the small nylon house and into their sleeping bags. Jason realized it was not going to be as comfortable and warm as his own bed, but he was just glad to be horizontal – his legs told him so.

Within minutes, the sounds of croaking frogs and toads, the splashing of water on the rocks and other foreign sounds kept Jason awake and wondering what hairy monsters were lurking around outside the tent. The same sounds seemed to put his dad to sleep.

The next sounds Jason heard were birds chirping and the whistle of loons on the lake. He also heard and smelled bacon crackling on the open fire waking up his stomach. Still in the clothes he wore yesterday, he put on his dirty shoes, made a quick trip to water another tree and joined his dad at the fire. Eggs scraped off a crusty frying pan never tasted so good.

Throughout the next three days at Frosty Point, as Jason named it, he and his father enjoyed fishing, hiking, and swimming in the icy water, and shared their hearts. Marc took advantage of this solitary time and explained to his son, now that he was twelve, his life was about to change big time because of physical and hormonal changes. He told Jason how these changes would affect his attitudes and feelings about other people, especially girls.

With not much to do, the two new buddies just spent time talking and sitting on logs around a fire in the center of a circle of rocks. Off to the right side, about ten feet away, waves from Frost Lake splashed on the rocks. In the distance, the quiet cove was bordered by a long stretch of golden sandy beach.

Suddenly Marc broke up Jason's thoughts. "Jay, things are going to change all over your head, and it's important that you be ready to change with them and know what's going on inside your hide. Kids usually learn these things from the streets or their friends, like I did. Most of the time the information is all bent out of shape and it takes half a lifetime to get it right. I want to clue you in straight."

"Like what stuff?" Jason said warily.

"Take sports, for instance. As a player and now an assistant football coach at the high school, I realize that the lessons we learn on the field about fair play, setbacks, hard work, effort, and success all apply to daily life in whatever you do. 'Pull your own weight,' 'There ain't no free lunch,' 'It's not all about me,' are more than just cute sayings. They're attitudes you should put in your head and live by.

Those expressions are how you should treat other people you live and work with, like neighbors, teachers, employers, friends, girls, and your own mother."

Jason nodded his head slowly. *Never thought of all that. I guess other people are important.*

Chapter Five

During the time at Frosty Point, Marc brought up some subjects that Jason was surprised to hear from his dad. Personal things that were so deep he thought they shouldn't be talked about. The biggest mystery that was cleared up in his mind was why his birthday came only seven months after his folks' anniversary. For the past few months, something had begun to gnaw inside his head after last year's anatomy chapters in his health book.

"Jay, I want you to know something about yourself, and I want to be the one to tell you before you pick up the dirt from someone else."

"Yeah? What's that?"

"Let me get right to it. You know how long it takes a baby to form in the mother, don't you?"

"Sure, nine months, right?"

"Right. Have you noticed that your birthday is only seven months after our anniversary?"

Jason counted month to month on his fingers. "Yeah, seven months. I guess I was – what do you call it? – a preemie?"

"No, son, you were full term."

"Well, that means ..."

"Yes, Jay, you got your start before your mom and I were married."

Jason opened his mouth, closed it, and then opened it again. "You and Mom — ?"

"Listen to me, son. Our emotions got the best of us before we were married, and I've regretted it ever since. Before I became a Christian things like that happened. I didn't seem to have any reason to control my own selfish desires. Since I've become a Christian, thanks to our friend John Carlson, I've come to know my sin as it really is. I've had to confess all this to a lot of people, first to your mom, our parents, and now to you. Our sin is something we can't hide. At some point everybody figures it out."

"Why do you call what you did a sin? It goes on all the time on TV and in the movies."

"That's the point. The world winks and makes fun at sex before marriage, but God calls it sin. I didn't look at it as sin when it happened. I got taken with all that TV stuff too. I knew it wasn't right, and there was a risk of a child. It embarrassed all of us a lot. The news, 'We're going to have a baby,' was not the happy occasion it should have been.

"Abortion was a legal option. But your mom went to a crisis pregnancy center, and a wonderful lady named Jan told her how you weren't just a blob of tissue that could be tossed away. In Psalm 139 the Bible says that God has every day of every life fully planned from conception. Some friends even suggested we have an abortion, and no one would ever know."

Jason could feel his mind searching for something. Then he got it. "Abortion means stopping the growth of a baby. It means killing the baby, doesn't it?"

"That's right, son."

"No one would know, would they? I mean, you don't

have to go around telling people."

"After just a few weeks of carrying you, your mom couldn't even *think* of getting rid of you. Thanks to Jan at the pregnancy center, we decided we'd face up to our mistake. She convinced us you were just as much Jason Greene at three weeks as you are Jason Greene now – right here at this camp fire, although of course we didn't know your name then. Not even if you were going to be a boy or a girl. When I think of what we almost did, I literally get sick to my stomach. We had a quick wedding, and it really tore up your grandparents. Some of your older cousins have figured it out and have asked about it. It makes it tough for your aunts and uncles to answer them."

"Why are you telling me this now, Dad? Can't we all just forget about it?"

"It doesn't work that easy. It's a memory I'd like to forget, but you're a constant reminder to me."

"Even after twelve years?"

"Yep. But you know, son, if that event didn't take place at that certain time and place, there wouldn't be you – Jason Marc Greene here with me right now at Frosty Point. I can't imagine my life without you."

"Dad, that's right – I wouldn't be here."

After a pause and some hard thinking, Jason said, "Does this all have something to do with me being an only child?"

"No. Your mom had three miscarriages after you were born. That's another story for some other time."

As Jason felt his eyes turning moist, he could see his dad's were doing the same. They studied each other's faces in intimate silence. Walking to the other side of the fire, a grown up and more understanding twelve-year-old stood behind his dad and put his arms around his neck. His dad took hold of his wrists and pulled him tightly to himself.

After a solemn and quiet moment, his dad grabbed him around the waist and dragged him up over his head like a sack of grain, plopped him onto the ground between his legs, and looked closely into his face. "I'd like to ask you – demand of you if I could – that you don't let your feelings run away and take over your emotions and actions like that, and hurt a girl and your families."

"I'd never do that, Dad. I promise."

"Remember what you've just said, son. You will be tested in very hard ways. Since I became a Christian I realize that God has canceled that sin out of my life, but there is no way of erasing the scar."

Jason got up, walked around on the sandy ground and asked, "A scar?"

"Like a scar that always shows from a wound on your body, sins leave scars on a life. Yes, forgiven and healed, but still scars."

"I think I get it. You're saying that sometimes the leftovers of a sin can't be hidden."

"Right on. There will be hundreds of temptations that will claw their way into your life, but remember, with every sin there is a consequence – a scar that will remain even after you become a Christian and give your life to the Lord."

"Well, I'm your son. So aren't I a Christian too?"

"No, Jay. Just because you're my son, doesn't make you a Christian. Everybody must make that choice themselves when they're ready."

"Will I do that some day? Like you? Become a Christian?"

"Jason, I pray for that every day. With all you have in front of you at your age, it's my prayer you will soon invite the Lord into your heart as Savior. But that has to be your own choice, at your time. I'm not going to push you into it.

Christ won't ever force you. It will be your decision."

"Is that what changed your life?"

"Have you noticed?"

"Sure, you used to lose your temper, swear all the time, and drink. Now you don't swear, and there's no booze in the house. Can't a Christian swear or drink?"

"The Christian life isn't a bunch of don'ts. As a Christian I just don't feel the need to swear or drink. Neither of them makes life any better. In fact, now I see how those things cheapened my life and made living tough for everyone around me."

"I thought it was fun to drink beer. It looks like that on TV."

"There ya go again, son. See how you're taken by all that TV and movie stuff? That's one of the worst messages advertisers dish out to you kids. The truth is, drinking leads to more misery than you and I could imagine. Broken homes, absent dads, innocent people killed or badly hurt in accidents, loss of jobs, money not spent on the needs of a family, fights, and lost friendships. A guy can live a long and happy life without all that garbage."

"I never heard of all that."

"You're proving my point. Of course you haven't. The modern world wants to hide under all the phony lies. Keep thinking for yourself. Since I've given up my old life, everything I know and feel has been better for you, your mom, and me. I honestly hope you never become involved in all that stuff."

"I won't, Dad. I promise."

"Son, when you become a believer, Satan will fight you every way he can. Every temptation that comes your way will test your future, family, and faith. He'll use doubt, ignorance, stupidity, peer pressure, and your hormones. The more you trust Christ in your life, the harder Satan will lean on you. He doesn't give up. The good news is that the Lord doesn't give up either. Keep this in your head, Jay: the battle is the Lord's, and He's already won it. Your job – to believe it."

From the flickering light of the fire burning between them, Jason could see his own reflection in his father's eyes, and he guessed his father could do the same. It was as if each of them was within the other.

His father continued. "When Satan dumps on you in the years to come, remember what we talked about here this week. While we're on these subjects, a wasted mind from drugs, bad lungs from smoking, even the hurts from a cross or evil-spoken word can mess up lives. Gambling also destroys a character. All these vices have less to do with being a Christian than they do with just simple good health, respect, and common sense. Above all, son, I want you to grow up to be an honorable man for your family and country. It won't be easy, with the enemy always pounding on you."

"I promise to remember all this, Dad."

"Those are heavy promises for a twelve-year-old to make."

"I'll do it for you, Dad. Just watch."

Throughout the days at Frosty Point, Marc and Jason wrestled with intimacies that only a father and son could, and the two came to trust and understand each other more and more. They bonded into a relationship neither of them had known a week before.

"Let me clue you in on something else I wish I had known when I was twelve," Marc said. "You'll always have struggles in life. Things will not always be fun and games like they are today. Think first. Hold your tongue. Stand on solid ground. You'll not always have all the answers – no one does. Just because you'll find yourself in conflict at times, doesn't mean you'll have to like it. See it through – deal with it. Situations change, son. It won't always be like it is at the time."

The hours and days of counsel and prayer were laced with swimming in water that never got above the feeling of ice, fishing with less and less success, and Jason learning to paddle the canoe alone and doing it right.

Several times he tried the canoe-lifting trick, but failed. "I promise I'll do it next year, Dad. You watch."

The two close friends were having such a good time alone they were hoping it could go on forever with no one to interfere. Not to be. The last night was upon them, and another experience was coming that Jason would never forget.

The far northern Minnesota weather was acting up as usual in its own way. While it had been hot and muggy at the start of the trip, it was now raining and in the low 50s. As they settled in for the last night, the temperature fell to the mid 40s by tent time. The fire flickering in the center of the rock circle did little to warm the campers.

"Now I know why I've called this Frosty Point." Jason said.

He couldn't stop shivering from head to foot in his sleeping bag, even wearing all the clothes he brought. His dad said he felt cold too, but said he was sorrier for his quaking, frosty-eyed son.

"Jay, this is one of those times that you cannot do anything about. Ya have to deal with it, handle it, you know, no choice, no option —"

"Yeah, I hear ya, Dad, no other way. I can do it."

Marc said, "These sleeping bags can be put together as one, you know."

"Yeah, I know – I'll be okay." After thinking a little on that, "Ah, how do you do that, Dad?"

"The zippers will join each other, but we'll be together."

"Yeah, I think we should."

The adjustments were made quickly, and soon they were in their cocoon.

"Kinda weird, huh, Dad?"

"Yep, but who's to know."

"I'm not tellin'. No one should know about this, huh?"

Jason wondered if he would ever be this close to his dad again. Did older boys let their father's keep them warm at night while they shivered? Probably not, and even if they did, they'd never let on. Who could know what the future held? Jason squirmed at first, but the warmth led him to relax. Sleep slowly engulfed both of them while the cold unthinkable and unpredictable future swirled and blew around outside the little nylon house.

Throughout the ordeal of getting up early, eating pancakes that looked more like scrambled eggs, they packed up, doused the fire one last time, canoed over three lakes and portages, and did it all in crusty week-old dirty jeans. Feeling like an experienced eighteen-year-old tough guy, Jason was on top of it all. When they got to the rapids between Skoop and Ada Lakes, his father let him make the decision as to walk up through the rapids or portage around them, like he said he would a few days ago. Jason chose to portage, which he quickly regretted.

There was no path like they were used to, and the trees and underbrush were so dense they had to cut down small trees and both carry the canoe through on its side. Mud, bugs, mosquitoes, soggy ground, and boulders made the trek almost impossible. Tree branches scrapped and scratched arms, legs, and faces. Jason knew he had never sweat so much in his life, and his stiff dirty clothes stuck to him like plaster. The distance was only about five hundred feet, but the three trips they had to make took two hours.

Jason figured his dad was helping him learn another lesson in life as he was watching him battle the unforgiving experience. He could sense his dad was thinking about him. Just then Marc said, "Jay, I've never been more proud of you. You did all that without complaining."

"Well, Dad, maybe you're getting through to me. No choice, no option, no other way. You know how it goes."

At the end of the ordeal they both took off their clothes and shoes and jumped into the lake. After the dip in the cold water, even a change back into dirty but dry clothes felt good.

Like two new buddies they talked all the way back about next year's canoe trip to the same place.

"In the future," his father said, "maybe you'd like to bring a friend or two along and enjoy all this with them."

Jason stopped paddling for a while and kept looking ahead taking at the wide expanse of glistening blue water reflecting the sky and white clouds. With a deep breath of pure clean air he twisted around, and rested his elbows on the gear.

Connecting eyeball to eyeball with his father, he said, "I don't think so, Dad. Let's call these trips just our time together."

He could feel a new sensation of warmth and love radiate between them, and he felt a fresh new appreciation for the man he lived with, but hadn't known until now.

"Jay, Jay, – Jason! It's me. Chris. Chris Young. Don't

you hear me?"

The voice of his best friend from school demolished the enjoyable memories of the canoe trip, brought him back to the porch, his corner post, and the horrific reality of the day.

Chapter Six

Chris Young, Jason's chunky, freckled faced, red headed friend, had just come through the kitchen door and was heading towards him with a look of sadness for his friend. "Boy, you sure were in another world. I called you a coupla times before you came around."

"I was thinking about the canoe trip Dad and I took last year. We were planning another one for next month. Did I tell you about it?"

"Only a few hundred times. We just heard about your dad, and my mom thought I should come over. I don't know what to say. But you know my grandpa died just three weeks ago, so I kinda think I know how you feel. It must be worse for you though."

"You don't have to say anything, Chris. And I'm glad you care and came over."

"Wanna play catch?"

"Na."

"Ride bikes?"

"Na, I can't, 'cause my bike's busted."

"Want me to call some of the other guys?"

"No, I just want to be alone and quiet for now. You can stay."

They sat on the steps of the porch throwing little stones to the centerline in the driveway. In a few minutes Chris said again, "I'm sorry. I just wish I knew what to say."

"Don't worry about it. I wouldn't know what to say either. It's just nice to have you here. Think I'll ever be happy again?"

"I 'spose. People get over these things. I did, when my grandpa died."

With a bite in his words, Jason said, "But this is my *dad*, Chris, not just a grandpa."

"Sorry."

Just then Jason saw his neighbor John Carlson come out of his house and start toward his garage.

"Sorry about what I did to your new car," Jason called to him.

"Don't let it bother you, Jay. Your bike suffered more."

"Hey, where is my bike? I don't see it."

"It's in my garage. I'll fix it for you."

"You don't have to do that, Dad will fix —"

Even with Chris looking on, Jason again found himself weeping in the grip of his neighbor.

"As for the scratches in the hood, we lucked out on that. Remember the hailstorm we had two weeks ago? I get a new hood from the insurance company. I'm just waiting for my turn at the body shop."

Two days later, Jason heard that his dad's body had arrived at the Alvin Funeral Home in Prairie Heights. Visitation was scheduled for Friday evening. On Thursday, Chris came to Jason's house again and they sat on the back porch where they found the solitude that suited them, and Jason asked Chris what goes on at a visitation.

"I remember a bunch of people came and stood in line

for a long time. They said nice things to our family, and then just sort of looked at Grandpa lying in the casket. It's like … a sad time for everybody."

Jason could feel the thought of his dad in a casket burning in his chest. He tried to work up the nerve for Friday evening.

On Friday, his father's two brothers, Joel and Jeff, their wives and children – Jason's five cousins – met him, his mom, and a small group of family and friends that included John and Karen Carlson, at the funeral home an hour before the visitation. Rev. Larsen and the funeral director spoke to the little cluster of people. Some officers and men from Marc's unit in the National Guard had returned from Minnesota and joined them.

Jason moved with the small group from the room to a larger room with a lot of chairs, soft music playing and a strong fragrance of flowers. At the far end of the room there seemed to be a wall of flowers and a casket in the center covered with a large United States flag. As they walked to the front, Jason squeezed his mother's hand and tilted his head to look at her for a clue how to react.

Stepping to the closed casket, they touched it gently, broke down in each other's arms and wept again. Jason heard sniffling and whispering behind him and never felt so heartbroken, empty, deserted, and alone – even in the midst of other family.

Before the funeral director let the other visitors in, Jason turned to the casket and stood looking at it for quite a while, not caring if the others were wondering what he was thinking. Rob and his two other uncles came and stood with him.

"How do I really know Dad is in there?" Jason asked,

while still looking ahead.

"I'm sure your dad is in there," Uncle Joel said. "This is the way the military does it."

"Are you sure?"

"Trust me; your dad is in there."

"Why can't I see him? Chris saw his grandpa."

Uncle Joel sighed, as though this was a question too hard to answer this soon. Then he said softly, "Jay, the hard fact is that your dad died in a bad crash and you wouldn't want to see him now."

"Is he just in a bag?" Jason persisted.

Standing nearby, a corporal from Marc's unit asked if he could explain this to Jason. Uncle Joel nodded, yes.

"To tell you the truth, because of his injuries, your dad's body *is* in a bag. His dress uniform is freshly cleaned and pressed and lies on top of him. Nameplate, awards, ribbons, polished brass, and company patches are all in place. His hat is on his chest and shined shoes at his feet."

"Dad showed me how to shine shoes like he did."

"I was the one who was asked to shine your dad's shoes. I hope I did as well as you would have done."

"I'm sure you did, corporal," Uncle Joel said.

"Thank you, sir," Jason said in a struggled whisper cracking with grief and broken by painful emotions.

The corporal leaned toward Jason, and whispered, "I have his boots in my car. After I clean the mud off, I'll give them to you."

"Don't take all the mud off," Jason said.

"Remember him like you saw him the last time you were together," Uncle Jeff said. "Remember all the good and fun times you had with him like on that canoe trip last year. You're really going to have to tough it up and become a strong man for your mom. Can you handle it, Jay?"

"Yeah, I can. Thanks, Uncle Jeff." Quickly Jason thought, *Here comes that tough it out stuff that Dad talked about on the canoe trip.*

At six o'clock visitors began to enter the big room. Jason could not believe the number of people who were in the long line. Friends from church, neighbors, people from all over town, and the mayor and his wife. There were teachers from all the schools in Prairie Heights and some other towns, many of his school friends, and a lot of National Guard friends of his dad.

Jason watched as all the military people saluted slowly at the casket before they came to see him and his mom Michelle. There were a lot of old guys wearing army caps full of decorations that Jason didn't know.

This show of respect for his dad made him feel proud – very sad, very hurt, but very proud. The outpouring of respect and care he saw that night would surely be one of many lessons and experiences he would never forget. The memory of the canoe trip a year ago and the canceled trip for this year kept sweeping over his mind. *I guess this is one of those things Dad said I would have to handle without him. No choice, no option, no other way. Just like carrying a heavy load over a portage, or a real cold night in the woods.*

For several hours people passed by the casket and said many fine and wonderful things about his father. Jason wished he could remember everything he heard. He was thankful for all of them, and his uncles told him how proud they were of him.

"You did very well tonight, Jay," Uncle Rob said. "You stayed with your mom for almost four hours."

"I thought I had to. They all waited for such a long time to see us. I thought I should be there for them. Some were really crying."

"You're learning your lessons well, Jay. You'll be tested hard at the funeral tomorrow."

Chapter Seven

That night, all aunts, uncles, and cousins were spread throughout the Greenes' and Carlsons' houses and back porches. Sure, they rested, but no one in either house got any good sleep.

Early the next morning, his two aunts, Carol and Konnie, Joel and Jeff's wives, along with Karen, John's wife, were the first up and prepared a good breakfast for all the others. Everyone got up at different times and had a breakfast buffet on the Carlsons' large back porch.

The funeral was scheduled for ten AM. At nine o'clock Jason heard a car from the funeral home arrive. When he went to look, he saw an officer from the Illinois National Guard also arrive and come in to greet Michelle and Jason.

"As we discussed the other day, military custom requires me to be your escort, Mrs. Greene."

"I understand, but I'd rather have Jason escort me."

"Very well, I'll be right behind you."

"Thank you."

The ride to the church was heartrending and quiet. Jason just held his mother's hand.Entering the large foyer of the church, Jason saw the flag-draped casket surrounded by four smartly dressed soldiers standing at attention at each corner. Each held a different flag – a United States flag, an Illinois State flag, the National Guard flag, and the flag of his father's own unit. After another brief moment for the family and relatives at the casket, they were ushered into a large room to wait for the funeral to start.

Everyone from the family found chairs to sit in, while most of the cousins just milled around. From a window in the room to the foyer, Jason watched another long line of people stop at the casket for a minute as they came into the church. Some just stopped for a second or two, and some knelt and crossed themselves. All military, police, and firefighters saluted the casket; again in a slow motion method.

A small unit of an army brass ensemble played soft hymns and traded off with the large organ as hundreds of people gathered into the large church. Jason saw many of the same people he'd seen the night before, including some older men with fully decorated soldier hats. Even the governor of the state, with his wife and a state patrolman, were with the mayor and his wife.

At the sight of the governor, Jason felt his Uncle Joel standing close behind him, with his hands resting on his shoulders. Jason let his uncle slip his arms down to his chest.

"Your dad meant a lot to these people," Uncle Joel said quietly. "Don't forget: promises kept, hard work, fairness, and kindness will always be remembered, respected, and honored."

Jason nodded his head slightly in agreement, and leaned back against his uncle.

Shortly after ten the church was full, and the large family group assembled to walk into the church. They all stood by as eight soldiers slowly marched to the casket, stopped, and turned to face it. With white gloves, each took hold of the handles under the edge of the flag and slowly lifted the casket and stood at the doors waiting to enter.

From the rear of the church, Rev. Larsen began the service with the words of Jesus. "I am the resurrection and the life. He who believes in me will live, even though he dies; and whoever lives and believes in me will never die. Do you believe this?"

The ministers, followed by the soldiers bearing the casket started down the aisle to the tune of *Nearer, My God, to Thee*, played by the brass ensemble. The funeral director motioned for Michelle, Jason, and the escort to follow the soldiers. The rest of the families walked in after them.

When everyone was seated, Jason looked to his right and found himself so close to the casket he could see the little white stitches in the red stripes, and smell the clean cotton scent of the flag. Being so close to his dad, his mind again drifted back to Frosty Point and that final cold rainy night on the canoe trip when he fell asleep in his father's arms.

The music stopped, the large doors at the rear of the church were opened again and the foyer filled with more people. The funeral began. Jason slid his hand up under the flag and stroked the edge of the casket. When he noticed no one else could see what he was doing, he left his hand there during the entire service.

At the close of the benediction, an hour later, with the organist playing *Amazing Grace*, the eight soldiers came back to the casket. They carried it to the rear of the church with Jason and his mom following. This time Jason saw an ocean of faces including neighbors, teachers, buddies, people he never knew. Most eyes were moist and blinking as they looked right back at him, including his Junior High friends, Chris, Tim, Sharon, Mark, Andy, and Shawn. Some wiped their eyes and some turned or bent their heads to avoid eye contact with him. The long, slow walk seemed to go on without end.

Finally stepping outside, Jason watched the scene with a surreal and numb feeling. Everyone involved did their job without a sound. The casket was carefully placed in the hearse while the four flags, held straight by the soldiers, whipped and snapped in the brisk breeze. Policemen from cars and motorcycles with pulsating and twirling red and blue lights, had all traffic stopped on Main Street.

Small cars and large trucks waited patiently in quiet respect as red and green traffic lights continued their work in vain, undaunted by the emotions all around. A heavyset bearded truck driver in his bib overalls stood outside his cab in a salute. Car doors closed softly and all sounds of the town were muffled in Jason's ears. Even a freight train traveling by at the north end seemed to have a quiet whistle and wheels.

Because his dad was also a member of the Prairie Heights Volunteer Fire Dept., two large fire trucks led the procession two miles to the cemetery, also with flashing lights. People from all over town stopped what they were doing and gently waved to the hearse, to Jason, and his mom.

Upon arriving at the entrance to the cemetery, four policemen on motorcycles pulled off to the side, stood at attention and saluted as the hearse and family drove through the gates. As the slow-moving line of cars wound its way through the trees and stones to the gravesite, Jason could see ahead the same waving flags, and the eight soldiers standing at attention where the rear door of the hearse would stop. Jason was impressed and full of pride. *Everything is so perfect, right on time and so sharp. Dad, you'd be proud of your men.*

The casket was placed on the framework over the grave while he, his mom, and his dad's brothers, sat in a few prepared chairs. The great group of people from the long procession gently closed car doors and stood behind the family in a large circle. Again a brief service followed.

At the end of the service, the first of twenty-one rifle shots rang out making Jason and everyone else jump. Jeff Swanson, a neighbor and first chair trumpet player in the high school band played *Taps* perfectly from a distance back in the cemetery where it echoed among the trees. As the music faded into silence, Jason and his mom held their arms around each other listening only to chirping birds and whipping flags.

Jason watched with a hollow heart as the soldiers at the casket folded the flag neatly into a tight triangle and passed it to the chaplain, who stepped to his mom and him, and said, "This flag is presented to you on behalf of a grateful nation and the United States Army as a token of appreciation for your loved one's honorable and faithful service."

Both Michelle and Jason nodded without a word. With tight lips and a hard face holding back a volcano of emotions, Jason accepted the flag with his mother.

Soon the ministers faced Jason and his mom and said a few personal words. Jason stood to attention as the governor stepped up, hugged his mom, then took his right hand.

"Young man, I knew your dad personally. We worked on some projects together. He was everything a good man should be. Son, be very proud of him, and follow his example for your life."

Looking up at the governor, Jason quietly said, "Thank you, sir, I will."

A few others came to the family to speak some final words, then drifted off to their cars and drove away. Jason realized he was left alone with his mom, embracing the flag. They stood one last time at the casket, and then joined with the whole family in one great hug.

Finally Jason completely broke down, losing his strength and composure. In a daze, he was only partly aware of his older cousin, Keith, helping him to the car.

Chapter Eight

Jason's fourteenth birthday on July twenty-seventh, two weeks after the funeral, came and went like a dull thud. When most boys his age thought only of football and skateboards, Jason, on his back porch with his post, was learning tough lessons of life: Life isn't fair; Life is down-right fragile and must be handled with care and respect. Jason spent long hours trying to put some form and color into the empty visions of the future and thinking over the promises he remembered making to his father.

A lot of rebuilding was going on in the lives of Jason as well as his mother and the Carlsons. His mother missed Marc for his special looks, warm physical presence, his wink, secret remarks and touches. Jason missed the trust and assurances of his dad. He missed his companionship, openness, approachability and counsel, especially after the canoe trip. He even missed his impatience at times.

John and Karen Carlson missed him for his friendship and sense of humor. John missed him as the brother he never had. Karen was a great help to Michelle by just being a good listener and a set of arms to collapse into when memories ganged up on her. John reached out to Jason in as many ways as he could without stepping into Marc's place.

Out of the blue, one evening at the kitchen table with the empty chair in their midst, Jason suddenly looked at his mom as a question burst into his mind. And he had to ask it. "Mom? Are you a Christian?"

"I became a Christian ...," his mom started with halting words, "... when I was seven years old in Bible School, with the help of Miss Anderson, my teacher. I grew up in the church and was active in many groups and the youth choir. In high school and college I drifted away from the Lord. Last year when John Carlson led your dad to the Lord and his life changed, I too reclaimed Jesus as my Savior. It was like a new and fresh start in our lives. I'll always be thankful to John for bringing your father to the Lord. Now I'll be with him again someday in heaven. We'll all be together when you become a Christian."

"When will I be a Christian?"

"At the time you're ready to ask Him into your heart."

That's the same thing Dad said, Jason thought, while staring out the window.

Jason's mother supported him in the "man-of-the-house" role by asking his advice on a number of things – even though he guessed that she knew. Together they would fix and repair little things around the house. At times in the midst of a little repair job like readjusting the flusher thing on the toilet or a broken spring on a door, mother and son would openly breakdown with Marc on their minds. Jason soon learned to wipe off a sniffle and tell himself, *I can do this, I really can. No choice, no option, no other way.* These were times when he knew the canoe trip had paid off.

It was a blurred time for Jason. For a few weeks many people were coming and going around the house doing things and keeping him busy. Soon that grew thin, and in about the third week the absence of his dad began to set in like a load of bricks on his heart. To add to the hollow feeling and pointless future in his chest it was a year since the canoe trip to Frosty Point, and the time he and his father would have been there again. And now other doors were opening up in his life, as the new school year was about to start.

For several years Jason had looked forward to the annual father/son football barbecue rib and burger night that was held at the Prairie Heights High School practice field at the start of the football season. This was to be the highlight of his freshman year because his dad was one of the assistant coaches. Now he wasn't sure he wanted to go to the picnic or even play football at all. The shine, sparkle, and purpose had been sucked out of his heart.

Three days before the barbecue he was with his neighbor John Carlson in the driveway shooting hoops like they often did, even before his dad's death.

"Jay, going out for football when school starts?"

"You know I always wanted to. But I don't know – I don't feel like it now, and Dad won't be there."

"What do you think your dad would say about this 'I don't know' decision, or no football, just because he isn't here? You know, he was looking forward to you wearing his same number."

"Yeah, I know." He took another long shot and only heard a "swish" as it fell through the net. "I 'spose he'd want me to go out. But the big barbecue rib and burger night is coming up in three days, and I don't want to go with just some other guys."

John shot the perfect air ball. "I'd like to go with you, if you'd let me."

Laughing at the big miss, "Would ya? Really? I'd like

that if you could make it. I know you're busy at the office."

Roughing up Jason's hair, John said, "I'm here for you, Jay. I'd consider it an honor. Look, we have to work with each other, friend. I don't have a son and you don't have your dad. Let's make a deal; I need your help too."

The two new buddies high fived each other and Jason ran into the house to tell his mom the good news.

The night of the barbecue wasn't so bad after all. John mingled with the other fathers, while Jason and the football hopefuls outdid each other with the BBQ sauce on the ribs and burgers stacked on the buns. Jason watched the older players use the occasion to gorge themselves, so he joined in. *Mom's not around*, he thought. The other men and boys were all aware of the awkward situation Jason was in, and they made him the center of attention. At the same time he realized another of his dad's lessons was being taught – and caught. Get up and carry on.

JT, another freshman kid in school without a dad was there. He and his mother arrived in Prairie Heights when he and Jason were in the fourth grade. Becoming one of the guys and getting a social foothold with other kids was always a tough job for him. JT said he'd also been looking forward to football when he got to high school. He rode his old bike to the barbecue and Jason spotted him there alone. He began to feel a certain connection with JT who was often in trouble with authorities, although Jason was well aware that others warned him to keep his distance from the boy.

When Jason and JT stepped up to get a burger off the grill, JT dropped his on the ground. Jason offered his burger to him only to be met with, "I can get my own." JT kicked the other burger under the grill. "Let some rat enjoy that one."

Chapter Nine

The next Monday morning at seven AM, lessons of football and life began in earnest, with the rookie football wannabes gathered in the senior high football locker room with all the coaches. Jason felt a mix of amusement and awe as he saw his own buddies looking like a scrawny crowd of adolescent heroes perched on the large benches, like a flock of birds on a telephone wire.

"It's the same funny little picture every year," he heard one of the coaches say to another. "Little plucked chickens trying to look like a football team."

The boys filled the room with chatter about how each of them was going to change the fortunes of P.H.H.S. and themselves. They talked how they all wanted to be quarterback, wide receiver or running back and make the headlines. Few spoke of being a defensive player – other than Andy Peters and Jason's best friend Chris Young. Jason thought those two could make up the defensive line all by themselves.

One of the coaches rose up to cut off the bedlam. "Listen up! Pipe down! Lesson number one in this room is when any of us coaches speak, you listen and listen quick! We don't repeat ourselves. The head coach of our school is the coach of all of us. He's going to give you kids the lowdown of what he expects from all of you starting today, right here, right now, right where you sit."

Another coach picked up a black pen and wrote, C-O-A-C-H on the white board. "That's him, Coach, and he wears the name proudly. He's been here so long no one knows his real name anymore. It's just Coach. He coached me and most of your dads when we sat on these same old benches – ten coats of gray paint ago. Like it or not, that makes him Grandpa Coach. Now hear this: the older boys will try and get you to call him 'Gramps.' You do, and you'll be the first to get acquainted with Mr. Bench real fast. Coach, you're on."

Suddenly, *"We're a team, not a bunch of players!"* a voice called from the back of the room. A stocky old gentleman looking more like Santa Claus than a coach kept talking as he made his way to the front. "The most important lesson remembered from a teacher is the first words the student hears from his mouth. And you just got yours. We're a *team*, not just a bunch of players. Put that into your DNA right now and don't forget it.

"This school has done well in recent years, and has a good reputation with three state championships and a lot of other good awards. Some players are in the state hall of fame, three of them in the NFL. I'm not living for the 'Coach of the Year Award,' I'm living to rise up good men for this town and country. I wake up every morning and come to work to build a bunch of guys like you into a team like a well-oiled machine. You'll need the same ideas of teamwork all your life – learn 'em now.

"I'm not one for cutesy little sayings, but I believe this one." On the white board he put the letters T-E-A-M in a vertical line at the left of the board without wiping off 'coach.' He wrote what each of the letters stood for. T = together, E = everyone, A = accomplishes and M = more. "Notice there is no 'I' in that word. Got that? Together, everyone accomplishes more. Looks dippy, doesn't it?"

Andy Peters bravely and loudly said, "Yeah!"

No one else said a word. He probably felt stupid as he looked around for help. The other guys all looked at the floor and each other, hiding their snickering.

"Good for you, young man. Don't be afraid to speak up. Hey, this team stuff works. It wins games. It works in football, on your job, and all the way through life." Leaning over the boys and pointing a stubby finger over the heads, Coach went on. "You will work, study, eat, and sleep like a team. If we see any 'hot dog'n' or 'look at me, Ma,' we probably won't yell at you, we'll just introduce you to Mr. Bench. You do get the idea that Mr. Bench is one of our best teachers, don't you? If you're the one who makes the touchdown or great sack, don't prance or dance around like God's gift to the sport, or Moses raising his hands to part the Red Sea – that's just your job. A high five will be enough. Bang each other around in the locker room, but *don't* puff yourself up in front of the crowd."

Coming off his gruff voice, Coach walked among the benches again, leaning over the kids. "Remember this team stuff, guys. In a machine every nut, bolt, washer, cam, arm, wheel, gear, leg, drop of oil, weld, and belt has its own job to do. If it's not there or gets rusty, or tries to do someone else's job, the machine – team to you guys – breaks down, gets broken, doesn't work, loses games.

"There is no unimportant player in football. Even the kid with the water is important; that's the oil to the players. This idea goes for your life in school, family, church, on the job, and in the military. Picking a connection here between football and life? You should.

"We promise you'll all play if we see you trying. We won't yell nasties or curse at you. I've never known a player of any sport who was inspired to do a better job by a ranting, swearing coach kicking furniture around a locker room. Threatened, embarrassed, ashamed or frustrated maybe, but not inspired. We coaches want to motivate you guys to do your best."

Jason sat glued to the bench with his friends. *Boy, this is all Dad stuff. This is just what he would say.*

Coach continued, "You know how to play the game. You've been through Youth Football, Junior High Football, played it in the streets and in the parks. You know the goals and the rules. Disappoint us and your best friend will be Mr. Bench. If you don't like something, or have a complaint – *tell* us. Don't talk behind our backs. We won't talk behind yours."

Jason discovered that Coach had a comfortable way of walking around the room while talking, even behind them at times. At other times he would speak right into the eyes of specific kids, the ones whose dads he knew when they had sat on the same benches. His large stubby and weathered hand often squeezed a young shoulder or two, leaving a feeling of trust and encouragement. Jason knew he was going to carry the feeling of a couple of those squeezes the rest of his life.

"Football is a tough game. It will teach you more about life than the game itself. Life will hit you harder than any player on the field. Some of you know that already. Some of you don't have a mom or dad in your life anymore for different reasons. You can feel sorry for yourself, find excuses, challenge authority, whine, whimper, or complain every day, but it won't change the fact. You'll have to see the situation for what it is."

He looked at Jason and glanced at JT. "In football and in life, you'll have to accept dumpy things and simply deal with them. Cope with them like a man"

Yes! Dad, Dad, Dad, went through Jason's mind.

"Carry this thought in your helmet, sons of Prairie Heights: character is built by the bricks and rocks thrown at you."

Returning to the front of the room, Coach put his foot on a bench. "Let's get back to football. You'll plan and practice plays until you'll know them in your sleep. They'll be perfect, but because of something called competition and opposition, they will fail.

"You'll get knocked down – get up.

"You'll be disappointed – go on.

"You'll work hard – work more.

"You'll get tired – keep going.

"Supposed to be in a certain place at a certain time? Be there.

"Want to argue with a referee? Don't.

"You'll make headway – then they'll push you back.

"You'll get leaned on by a coach – learn from it.

"And bury this in your DNA. Always expect the unexpected, and then the unexpected will be expected. That's football, men – that's life. Learn it now or learn it when you're fifty, but you *will* learn it."

Coach took a deep breath. "You guys have listened well. The benches need a break from your anatomy as much as you do. Get up, stretch and move around. Get a drink of water and say hello to somebody you don't know."

With a chorus of "Yes!" the boys all made a dash for the fountains and sinks. The babbling rose quickly and in typical locker room fashion, echoed between steel lockers and concrete floors. Jason saw a few guys say, "Hi" to JT, but little else. And no one spoke to him.

"Okay, take your seats," commanded one of the coaches. "Let's go on."

Jason saw little response or movement until another coach spoke up with the usual enthusiasm of an assistant coach cracking the plaster on the walls.

"Did you guys learn anything fifteen minutes ago about being quiet when a coach is talking? Wasn't it something like – how can I put it delicately? – *Shut up!*"

Coach started again. "Men, before we end our chat today there are a few final thoughts I want to leave with you. As these coaches start to mold you for your senior football team in a few years, respect them. Coaching freshmen football is a tough job, and they are not overpaid. Yeah, you know the game and the rules, but now start to put yourselves together as the team you want to be. These coaches will change a lot of your ideas. Listen to them. Sure, you all want to be quarterbacks, but some of you will have to play defense. Keep in mind, defense wins games too.

"Another thing you've got to learn as a team is responsibility. You, and you only, are responsible for yourself. Don't depend on mom or dad to do everything for you. Those days are gone. You're responsible for your equipment from shoes to helmet, and even that slingshot in the middle. Forget any part of that uniform – hello, Mr. Bench."

Coach was about to leave when he suddenly stopped and turned around. "Oh yeah, when we go anywhere in a bus, be there and be there on time. When the coaches get on, drivers go – they love us. In classes they take attendance, here we just go when it's time. It's a hard run to catch up." Leaning towards them one last time with eyes wide open and neck sticking out, "Don't laugh. Some guys have tried it."

They laughed.

Jason soaked up all this information and attitudes like a sponge. He could feel his heart get stronger. He felt ready and ripe for this strong male leadership he missed in the absence of his dad. He knew he was ready for football.

"Boys – I mean, men," another coach said, "line up alphabetically. You know where A, B, C belong. Do it on your own and see Mr. Stevens. He'll hand out your gear. Put it all in a locker and at one o'clock this afternoon we'll show you how to dress for the arena of your life."

Chapter Ten

His dad had been a teacher at Prairie Heights High School for as long as Jason could remember. As a four-year-old, he often played in the classrooms and sat at the teacher's desk with his feet dangling from the chair when his dad went to the school on a Saturday to do some work.

Entering the big sprawling brick building with high windows and ivy climbing the walls, his first day as a freshman somehow didn't have the excitement or anticipation most of the other kids seem to be experiencing. But he had an advantage in knowing where things were, and he felt good pointing out things to other freshmen.

Even though he felt sure about where he was, there was a silent hole in his heart because the one reason he looked forward to high school was missing. The first time he walked past room 114, where his dad had taught, and saw a new teacher writing something on the white board, he almost choked. *Tough it out, son,* echoed in his mind. He took a deep breath and quickened his step.

One thing that amused him, and gave him more assurance, was seeing the freshmen from small towns that had recently consolidated with P.H.H.S. They truly were a flock of lost sheep. Coming from their small buildings to this massive place was threatening and scary. Jason and his friends laughed at the sight of some of them clustered against the lockers near the office, afraid to move around. A teacher led them to their first hour class like the Pied Piper. Juniors and seniors were another story. They swaggered through the halls like royalty on their usual morning march. This was their place, their palace, their kingdom and no compassion was shown to the new flock. Not mean or nasty, Jason accepted the fact that they just controlled the atmosphere with a sense of superiority over the new "insects."

Almost as a relief, the bell rang for first hour. Jason and his friends parted to find their rooms. For Jason and his friend Tim Blake, known as the rich kid in town because his dad was the owner of the largest car dealership, it was room 218 and Freshman English. They mingled with others, and each found a desk to fit into.

Their English teacher, Eileen Riscoll, welcomed the new students with first day dignity and charm. "Good morning, class." Writing on the white board, she continued, "My name is Miss Riscoll. This is first hour Freshman English and I'm looking forward to my twenty-eighth and final year of teaching. I wanted to make it thirty years, but I don't think I have two more rounds left in me."

Jason stared, not knowing anyone could be that old or taught school for so many years. He remembered his dad talking about Miss Riscoll as a good, but tough teacher who had a funny way of shaking her finger at the students to make a point. It was her signature and trademark to hundreds of Prairie Heights alumni. She used that same finger to warn everyone on Friday. "Have a nice week-end, but be careful.

"The first order of business is getting you into your

assigned seats. As I call your last name, please sit in the seat I point to." Pointing to desk after desk, she said, "Abbot, Alford, Anderson, Blake, Cardosi, and Cook." She started the second row, DeSalvo, and ended with Greene. Miss Riscoll went on through the class list until she came to JT. "What's the 'T' for young man?"

"Just T," JT said.

"You must have a last name instead of just T."

"That's all there is. Just 'T'."

"Young man, I want to know what the T is for so I can place you in your proper seat."

"That's all you're gonna get. Just a T."

"If you are trying to get off to a bad start, you've done it. For the last time, what's the T for?"

Linda Anderson carefully raised her hand.

"Yes?" Miss Riscoll said harshly.

"He only goes by 'JT,' Miss Riscoll, – that's all any of us know."

"That's impossible," the teacher responded, in a voice that had clearly lost that first day charm she started with.

"But it's true, Miss Riscoll," Jason said. "He only goes by JT."

"We'll see about that. I'll find out."

"Good luck," JT said under his breath.

With steam about to blow from her twenty-seven years of well tuned ears, Miss Riscoll whirled around on her thick black heals, stomped back to the front of the room, and said, "I sure don't appreciate starting off the year with a challenge like this. *Sit here!*" she said, pointing her finger to a desk up front. She went on, "Taylor, Wade and West."

The rest of the hour passed with long and difficult introductions, handing out books and assignments. Jason heard Miss Riscoll mutter that she was never so glad to hear the bell at the end of the first day's class. "If students are becoming like this, I hope I make it out alive."

On his way out of the room, Jason paused at Miss Riscoll's desk. "He really does only go by JT. He always has. We've tried to find out, but we've only come up with JT. It's just been JT since he came to town in the fourth grade."

"You're Marc Greene's boy aren't you?"

"Yes, ma'am."

"I remember your father as a student of mine years ago. I'm very sorry about your dad's death this past summer. I've never been to a more moving memorial service. He was about the only decent male teacher and coach we had here. Let me add this. If I were you," she said, looking over the top rim of her classes, "I'd keep my distance from that JT fellow, or whatever he says his name is. He looks like bad news."

"Yes, ma'am."

In the early days of high school, Jason found a whole new world from middle school. New friendships developed with kids from other feeder schools, and he discovered the social ladder had a formal starting place – the bottom. In the lunchroom, for instance, the freshmen had to explore for their own territory. No fine real estate on the isles or by the windows. That property belonged to the juniors and seniors. In the locker room there was a fine line to tread to avoid the snap of a towel and other indecent threats.

The intrusion of Travis Valdez, a new freshman from California, upset the girl market. Travis came on the scene in mid freshman year when his parents moved to Prairie Heights and came to the little town with all the ego and looks of a Hollywood prima donna. Long sun-bleached hair and a clear bronze complexion that made the girls walk into open locker doors. He could even speak Spanish; or at least the freshmen thought it was Spanish. The guys saw him as nothing more than an over fashionably dressed arrogant pain in the anatomy that needed a lot of local humbling.

Mr. Arthur Melbourne, a Social Studies teacher tried to clue the newcomers to the school with some wisdom about learning.

"I'd like to tell you kids something as you start school. Don't be afraid to learn. I mean, ask questions and learn from your mistakes. You don't know this new stuff. What goes on here is 'learning.' Don't fight school. Use the time, the mistakes, and the failures to build your knowledge. We all learn more from mistakes than we do if everything goes right the first time. Scientists, inventors, engineers, athletes, doctors, and people from all professions will tell you that."

Tim Blake raised his hand. "You mean teachers don't get mad when we get things wrong and mess up some answers?"

"Exactly, Tim. Just keep an open mind and drink in the education you get. You'll never know when you'll need something you pick up here. I pass that pearl of wisdom to you all from experience. I struggled with school and ended up near the bottom of the class and barely snuck out of high school. It took me more than twenty years to learn what I just told you in three minutes."

At the close of the hour, Mr. Melbourne stopped Jason as he was about to go out the door. "I knew your dad for many years. He was a fun and kind of wild guy until he had some sort of religious experience. Then he became more serious, but more realistic. Follow his example, Jason. They call you Jay, right?"

"Yes, sir."

"Remember all you can about him. Keep your nose clean and we'll all be proud of you for him."

Thank you, Mr. Melbourne. I'll try to do that."

Chapter Eleven

The best part for Jason of starting the freshman year was being involved in football. He could quickly see that freshman football was full of blunders as he and the others tried to get the hang of playing as a team. The whole team stumbled and bumped into each other like the typical freshman football team. Every player still wanted to be the star and strength of the team, but it seemed some of them couldn't get the hang of being in the right place at the right time. Just the pride of strutting under big shoulder pads and clicking cleats filled young egos. All went well for Jason until the second away game, when he missed the bus.

That experience alone drove home what Coach told them on that first day –about missing the bus. Even though his mom and Karen Carlson raced to drive him to Ravenswood on that Saturday morning, it was too late and no use. When he arrived and joined the team in the locker room, no words of shame, apology, or confession could erase the sin of missing the bus.

"Sorry, Coach. Remember we had that power outage last night and the alarm clock didn't go off this morning."

"Right, we all suffered through that."

"I'll get ready." He jerked open a locker and threw in his

jacket.

"Hold on, Sparky; that translates into 'you missed the bus.'"

"Yea, but I'm here now, so I'll get ready." Jason continued to change clothes.

"Ready, yes, but sit the bench."

"Huh?" He stood there half in and half out of uniform, dumbfounded.

"You do remember what Coach said on day one about missing the bus, don't you? He and all of us mean what we say, and for your benefit learn it now. Clocks come with batteries, you know."

"But, Coach, I ..."

"No, 'But, Coach, I ...'" He pointed. "The bench!"

"I won't do it again. You know I'm always here."

With a set of eyes that looked more like the front end of a shotgun, the coach looked at Jason. "*Mr. Bench!*"

"Yes, sir."

While doing his duty by sitting the bench, he wanted to pout and feel sorry for himself, but could feel his dad slapping the back of his head, "*This is it, son, deal with it.*"

Other than that brush with disaster, Jason loved football because it gave him that outlet to run, yell, push others around, get dirty, and all those other fourteen-year-old thrills. In that freshman year he put on a growth spurt that added inches to his height, some more beef, broader shoulders, and muscle throughout his body.

One day after a particularly rough practice at his chosen position of tight end, Coach Sidney Towers pointed to a bench. "Greene, come into my office."

"Sure, Coach." Jason knew better than to call him Sidney.

"I was watching you out there today and you're not

getting it, are you?"

"No, I can't seem to twist myself and get out where I belong at the right time."

"Ever thought of playing defense?"

"No! Defense is for fat guys."

"Greene! You're not fat, but you've got good bulk, muscle, and brains to make a good defense player."

"Think so? Defense players need brains? They don't make the touchdowns."

"A lot of guys don't make the touchdowns. Defense players still win games, and a good one can make a miserable day for the opposition."

Jason sat glued to the bench looking down at the grass and digging a hole with his heel in the dirt at the edge of the field.

"As your coach, Jay, it's my job to get the best out of you and tell you where I think you'd be the best player for the team. Remember what Coach said on that first day about all being a great machine?"

"Dad and I always talked about being a wide receiver or tight end."

"Your dad was a sharp coach, but I don't think he knew how big and strong you'd be as a freshman."

"You knew my dad?"

"Sure did. We all did. That's why you and I are sitting on this bench – alone. I'm sure he'd like to see you become the best player of any position. With your football background and your heart for the game, you could be a strong leader in the defense as you go through high school and college."

Cocking his head and looking up at Coach, Jason felt a touch of his dad. "I'll try, Coach, but if it doesn't work can I go back to tight end?"

With a healthy high five, the coach said, "Deal."

Starting in the next four plays, it worked. Jason felt comfortably secure, knowing success in the new position. He found it a lot more fun breaking up plays and hitting others as part of his job. An eager defense player found a home in his chest, and he made up his mind never to look back.

The freshman team finished the season with a modest showing of six and three. In his desire to be the player his dad would be proud of, he really poured it on. In the last three games of the season the coaches let him play on both freshmen and junior varsity teams. At first the sophomore players whined and griped about a freshman player with them, but they soon found a place for the guy who did their job. Jason hit his stride in football – just at the end of the season.

JT was forced to give up football halfway through the season because he couldn't make some of the practices, and he missed the bus twice for away games. Jason tried to encourage him to stay with it, but he could see that there was just no way JT was able keep up. He even had difficulty in school work, and catching any rung of the social ladder was out of reach. When Jason, against the advice of Miss Riscoll and others, tried to talk with him, he had the usual answer. "Why do you bother with me, Greene? I don't want to talk about it."

"Just thought I could help ya."

"Well, save your charity for some other geek. I can make it on my own."

"Okay, okay."

When the football season was over in early November, and basketball proved beyond Jason's maneuverability and running endurance, he was glad to hang up all the practices and the fast pace of sports. Chris tried to get him to go out for wrestling for the winter season.

"I don't think so, Chris. I need something with short bursts of running in it. Maybe I'll take up some sport in the spring like track. I'd like to do that pole vault thing."

"You're kinda built for something like that. Me, I'd probably do the shot put. I sure can't run a lot."

Throughout the winter months, working out in the weight room helped Jason sweat, but school seemed to drag without the demands of sports. He felt content to pay more attention to doing better in school. At the same time a friend named Sharon Warwick, whom he had known since Happy Hands Preschool, began to look more interesting as she was walking onto his stage.

When he felt he was slipping in his grades, his mom would get on his case once in awhile. He knew that working in the office of the high school gave her the unfair advantage of hearing from his teachers too much for his comfort.

Then one bright day in math class, the canoe trip with his dad paid off again, when they were discussing weights and measurements and the subject of the rod came up.

"Anyone know how long a rod is?" Mr. Malcolm Williams asked.

The students all looked at each other, wrinkled up their faces and lifted their shoulders,

"What's a rod? Where is that ever used?" one of the students asked.

Raising his hand with a grin, Jason answered, "Sixteen-and-a-half feet."

In stunned silence, Mr. Williams and the students looked at him, clearly wondering how anybody knew that.

"How'd you know that?" Mr. Williams asked.

"Yeah," some of the other kids said, "how did you know

that?"

With somewhat of a flippant voice, yet missing a little of the Greene humility, he said, "In the Superior National Forest of northern Minnesota, the distance of the portages between lakes is measured in rods."

"Well, la-de-*dah*," Shawn said.

"Whoop-de-*do*," from Sharon Warwick.

"Nice work," Mr. Williams said. "You never know when or where you'll catch a morsel of wisdom as you traverse this sod."

Jason knew the math teacher seemed to enjoy embellishing his comments to stretch the students' thinking.

Chapter Twelve

For a reason he didn't fully understand, Jason somehow was able to hit it off and talk at length with JT, where other kids stayed away from any contact with him. Girls avoided JT like a disease, and guys turned him out of their groups. Jason often wondered why that was so, and one day it hit him. There was a missing link in their lives that connected them – a missing dad.

Prairie Heights High School was located on the far eastern edge of the Orlin Park subdivision. On a particularly warm January day, Jason was walking his usual three blocks home when JT in clothes, torn from wear not fashion, caught up to him in his daily trek to the apartment he lived in above the empty Ben Franklin Store on Main Street. Jason knew that JT would walk halfway, no, all the way, through town just not to be seen getting on a school bus he called a crummy yellow banana.

About one block into the walk, JT lit up a cigarette.

"Where'd you get that?" Jason asked. "You can't smoke."

"Oh yeah. Who made you the cop?"

"I didn't mean that. I mean you can't, or shouldn't, smoke till you're eighteen."

"Forget that rule stuff, Greene, I can get cigarettes any

time I want to."

"Do they really taste good?"

"Here, take one and find out." JT offered Jason the pack with a cigarette sticking out.

"Na, I don't think I should."

"Take it, Greene. It won't kill ya. Here, I'll light it for you. Let's get between these garages."

Huddled between two garages, Jason still looked in all directions.

"Put this end between your lips – not that far. Now, take a deep breath as I light it."

Sucking in a deep breath, Jason nearly choked. His tongue burned and his eyes stung instantly. "Plit, plit, plit." With a disfigured face and a cigarette wedged between two fingers, he said, "You like this? This is cool? You gotta be crazy."

Laughing out loud, "You'll get used to it, Greene. It comes easier with the next ones."

After a good try by sucking up the full cigarette, Jason said, "I don't think there'll *be* a next one. My lips, tongue, lungs, nose, and eyes are all telling me this is why I hear so much about not smoking. How much do you pay for this thrill?"

"I don't pay for these. Mom buys 'em by the carton and she lets me have a pack now and then."

With red eyes wide open and blinking in pain, Jason said, "Your mom?"

"Don't go freaking out on me. Yea, I get 'em from the old lady. No big deal."

"A little unusual isn't it? I mean your mom buying you cigarettes?"

"I 'spose so. Try another?"

"No way."

Roy Swanberg

Jason walked with JT, spitting bitter flecks of tobacco out of his mouth, with JT looking like he was enjoying the smoke. Jason thought a mouth full of peanut butter would kill the taste and the smell before his mother found out.

When Jason got home and was walking up the driveway, he saw John Carlson washing his car again. "It's three in the afternoon, Mr. C.; I thought you'd be working."

"That's one of the advantages of being a self employed lawyer. My time is my own."

As Jason walked closer to John Carlson, John sniffed the air. "Friend, you'd better bury that jacket somewhere for a while before you mother smells what I do."

"Huh?"

"Smoke, Jay. You've been too close to the smoking crowd."

"Oh, Mr. C., I think I've been closer to a smoker than you think."

"Tell me about it."

"A guy called JT got me to smoke a cigarette."

"Ouch. JT, huh."

"You know him?"

"I'm afraid I do. He would be one to stay away from."

"You too? Everybody says that."

"That tell you something?"

Jason had something deeper on his mind. "It wasn't right to smoke was it?"

"Smoking one cigarette doesn't make you an evil kid."

"I hope not. Dad and I talked about these things on the canoe trip, and I promised him I wouldn't smoke."

John dropped the sponge into the bucket and put his foot up on a bumper. "What did you learn from the trip to the other side just now?"

"Found out it tastes terrible and blisters the tongue. I

don't know why people smoke at all."

"You just learned the first reason why most people don't."

"I don't know why kids do it."

"Peer pressure, my friend, peer pressure. It works for all vices. 'I can do it if you can do it.' Say no to the first – or second – offer, and you'll be over the biggest hump of not smoking at all."

"Tough isn't it?" Jason figured out.

"Sure is, but you're getting tall and developing a good build." Laying a gentle fist into Jason's shoulder, "You can get away with a direct No! Others will get the hint. You'd better leave that jacket in my garage. Then get inside and have a peanut butter sandwich – or two."

Peanut butter? Guess I had the right idea. "Thanks, Mr. C."

Chapter Thirteen

In the springtime of his freshman year, Jason was feeling settled into the high school routine, comfortable with his place on the social ladder. Not up with the popular crowd and not on the bottom rung either. School work was okay and he was anxious to get back into some sport where he could run, yell, and throw his body around.

Track was the answer, and the pole vault pole just fit right into his large muscular hands. His upper body was developing well and he remembered the early hot days of the canoe trip where he first noticed his dad's broad back and shoulders. About six months ago he began to use the weights his dad had in the basement in an effort to develop better.

Jason was aware of Coach Towers watching his feeble attempts at the pole vault with a doubtful eye and a shaking head. "Greene, see that senior over there? Erik Whalberg. You know, that new kid from Washington State. Give him a chance to help you and listen to him. He can tell you a lot more about this than I can."

Why should I have to listen to him? I can jump with this stick on my own.

After trying a few lousy jumps and riding the pole off to

the side or ending in a heap on the ground in front of the airbag, it was time to eat some crow and talk.

"Ready to listen to Erik?"

"Yeah, Coach, bring him over here."

Coach Towers called Erik over to where he and Jason were standing. "See if you can say something to the *Greene* kid here about pole vaulting he doesn't know."

Erik started right in with, "I've been watching you for the past few days myself. Coach is right, there's a lot you don't know about this gig. If you don't stiffen your arms and make them a part of the pole, and let the pole do the work, you might as well call this a high jump with a stick."

Jason watched closely how Erik made three jumps – clearing over ten feet each jump.

Counting the steps back to the starting line, Jason grabbed the pole, ran forward, placed the end of the pole into the box, stiffened his arms and the bent pole lifted him up right into the bar at six feet.

"Good start, Greene." Erik Whalberg yelled. "Next time swing your feet up over the bar. That's the point of this game. Leave the bar on the poles."

"Yeah, yeah, yeah, I got it, I got it."

On the next attempt with his feet pointed skyward and his body upside down he wanted to let go and claim his rightful position in the human race. But he couldn't take any more of Erik's smart remarks, so he hung on and plowed right into the bar – again. "Don't say anything, Wally. I'll get it this time. I'm getting closer."

With another try, putting everything together, this time he cleared the bar and plopped into the air cushion on the other side. "See that? See that? Hey guys, see that? I pole vaulted."

Shaking his head in disbelief, Erik said, "Greene, you

just jumped over a six foot bar. High jumpers do that without the stick. Real pole vaulting starts at ten feet. Now all you have to do is the practice thing – over and over and over. You know the drill."

On Sundays after church it seemed half of the church-going crowd in town took their turn waiting thirty minutes in line for dinner at the Dawg Hause. Eating in a dog house didn't seem to be the proper place to enjoy a Sunday dinner, but the history behind this icon of Prairie Heights was a story everyone was proud to repeat.

About twenty years ago, Doug Hauseman, son of a single mother with cancer, dropped out of high school in his junior year. Shortly after that, his mother died. Drifting from pillar to post for over a year and some brushes with the law, Doug got a lowly job of sweeping floors at the Dog House. The Dog House was nothing more than a shack struggling to be called a restaurant, but it served as a hangout and drive-in on highway 6 at the west end of town.

Harry and Esther Stein, a childless couple who were deeply respected throughout town, named their little stand "The Dog House" in honor of the school mascot Earl, the Bulldog.

Finding his niche at the Dog House doing anything to help the Steins, Doug endeared himself to the couple to the point of son-like status. Within two years he literally became chief cook, waiter, dishwasher, bouncer, supervisor, and manager. When the Steins were both suddenly killed in an auto accident, Doug found himself sole heir to the Steins' entire estate – business, home plus furnishings, and over four hundred thousand dollars in securities.

Shortly after the Stein's deaths, Interstate 80 was completed just north of town, and business on west 6 began to turn into empty buildings, including The Dog House. With the help of Seymour Franklin, a local banker who knew of Doug's hard work and faithfulness to the Steins, Doug bought the empty Super Super Save store near exit 56 on the new interstate 80.

Mr. Franklin hired Lee Builders to renovate the store for Doug. He renamed the place "The Dawg Hause" and turned it into the great family restaurant it became. With good advertising locally and on Interstate 80 in both directions, The Dawg Hause was the favorite place to stop on that Chicago – Quad Cities trip.

On one particular Sunday, Jason, his mom, along with his chunky, freckled faced, red headed friend Chris Young with his parents and two sisters, were all enjoying dinner, when Doug Hauseman, owner and all around town ambassador stopped by their table on his appointed rounds.

"Everything okay here? Service, food and all?"

Full of food, all heads nodded approval.

"Everything's fine, Mr. Young," Chris's dad said. "By the way, rumor has it you plan to build on to this place. Any truth to that, Doug?"

"More than just a rumor, Jim. I'm going to expand off to the left and build a formal banquet facility. This town needs one, but my problem now is finding a good name to honor the Steins."

"The way things work out for you, Doug, I'm sure you'll come up with just the right name."

Jason shifted his seat so Doug could pull a chair up to the table and squeeze his mature figure between him and Chris. Putting one of his large hands on each of their shoulders, Doug said, "Hey, you guys, if you're looking for work sometime, I always need responsible and good working kids. I've watched you two grow up and you look the type."

Jason looked at each Chris, both with wide open eyes and mouths, then at their parents. Jason spoke first, "Mom, whaddya you think?"

"Sounds like a good idea, but there's a lot to think about and put together before you start. School, homework, sports. How are you going to get here, and other things."

"Spoken like a mom," Doug said, as he leaned into Jason and bumped his shoulder. "But she's right."

Jim Young said, "There's also the question of you two working on Sundays, Chris. You know how we feel about that."

Doug nodded. "Well, think about it folks. You too, girls, when you get older. Let me know. I'm always here."

On a Saturday afternoon at the end of the school year, Jason, Chris, Tim Blake, and Corbin Wallis were hanging out at Three Oaks Mall as they usually did when nothing else was going on. When they walked towards the mall, they noticed three police cars with lights on, parked by the main entrance. Just as they entered the building, the boys saw three policemen leading JT out in handcuffs.

Jason hurried towards JT. "What's going on?"

As JT started to answer, one of the officers roughly said, "Get back, kid. Don't come any closer," as he shoved JT into the car, banging his head on the top of the doorframe.

Jason stopped walking as Chris pulled his jacket. But he asked again, "What's going on?"

Yelling through the closing door, JT said, "Don't worry about it, Greene. My hands just got too sticky."

Another police officer came to the little group. "You're Marc Greene's kid aren't you?"

"Yes, sir, I am."

"Remember when you guys were little we came to your school and told you about shoplifting? This is what happens. If you know that kid, stay away from him. Now listen to us, will ya?"

Jason and the group of friends kept staring as the officers drove JT away. The small group, frightened and some shaking over what they had just seen, sat down on a nearby bench.

"I heard JT. shoplifted, but I didn't think it was true," Corbin said.

"He's always in trouble," Tim added.

Chris asked, "What's the deal with him anyway? Jay, you know him better than all of us. You even *talk* to him."

"He has a rough time with a lot of things. He had to drop out of football, and school's been tough for him."

"School is tough for lots of us. You feel sorry for him, Jay?" Corbin asked again.

"Well, he doesn't have a dad tha —"

"You don't either," Chris said. "How come you're not always in trouble like that?"

"Chris, I've got my mom who is always around, and the Carlsons have helped a lot. I even think the church and the Sunday school thing might be a reason. JT wouldn't be caught dead in a church. He doesn't have nice people to hang out with like we do."

"Hey, where *is* his dad? Divorced or dead? You should know, Jay."

"I don't know. He told me I'll never know. I guess no one knows, and never will."

Chapter Fourteen

With the experience at the mall, Jason was almost relieved when his freshman year came to an end. Summer vacations were always the highlight of every year, but this would be the second summer without his dad. Remembering the times he and his dad had enjoyed together in the summers, still gouged a hollow hole in his heart. The second canoe trip was not to be. No more good times in the future with Dad.

This year Uncle Joel and Aunt Carol who lived near Chicago invited him to spend the Fourth of July with them and his cousins, Keith and the twins Jessica and Jonathan. The cousins had the week planned with many things to do and places to go in the city. Jason had been there before, but only as a little kid. He didn't remember much other than the noise. This time the kids were all old enough to travel around alone. Keith was a senior in high school and the twins just a year behind.

From the time he stepped off the train in Union Station and met the cousins, Jason felt he was on another planet. Chicago and Prairie Heights were as different as Venus and Mars. Keith told Jason to stash his backpack in a locker, and they went straight to the Sears Tower.

"It's been sold to some other company," Keith explained,

"but to almost everyone in Chicago it will always be the Sears Tower."

The Jackson Street lift bridge across the Chicago River was up, and they had to wait over fifteen minutes, just so three sail boats with tall masts could go up river. As Jason looked up at the raised bridge in awe, he wondered what it would be like to climb the bridge railing while it was up. The cousins were bored by the delay. When they got to the Sears Tower and rode to the Sky Deck in the elevator, the usual wind in the city made for a clear day and a fantastic view. Jason could even feel the building sway.

Looking out from the floor to ceiling windows, Keith pointed out things in the city. "See, right down there is what we call the Loop. The elevated trains come in from the different areas of the city, make a loop and go back." Pointing to the north, he said, "Up there is Michigan Avenue and Lake Shore Drive. Look beyond that green forest-looking part and you'll see Wrigley Field."

"Wrigley Field?" Jason said with excitement. "Can we go there for a game?"

"We're way ahead of you," Jessica said. "We'll be there Thursday." She then pulled Jason to a set of windows sticking out from the building where they could stand on glass looking straight down.

"I don't like this," Jason said, "My gut tickles."

Jonathan brought Jason to the east windows. "The museum campus is over there and the planetarium is out on that point."

"What's that funny looking silver round building? It looks like a flying saucer," Jason asked with a wrinkled face.

"Look into the center of it. What do you see?"

"A football field. Hey, is that Soldier Field?"

Keith nodded enthusiastically. "Yep. Home of Da Bears."

"Wow, where do we start?" Jason said, wanting to get out of the swaying tower.

"First we go back to the station, get your backpack and take it to another station where we take a train to Wheaton where we live. We'll start tomorrow."

Jason felt the ride down in the elevator displace his internal organs.

Every morning for the next week they climbed on the train at Wheaton with the other daily commuters, traveled through suburbs and city again to Ogilvie Station. Like young kids they walked to the major museums, rode the ells, subways, trolleys, and double deck buses. Jason thought it would be a fun job to drive one of those trolleys around the city.

Jason got the feeling that walking and running on the lake front, and having a great day at Navy Pier, made his life seem somehow fuller. A big event going on in Chicago that week was the *Taste of Chicago*. At the *Taste* Jason ate his full of all kinds of food. *If I live through this day, I won't eat for a week.* On the way out of Grant Park he couldn't believe there were so many people in the world, and the traffic was awful. Cars, SUVs, vans, and buses were curb to curb. It looked like a gigantic parking lot with people just sitting in their cars. Jason wasn't surprised to find out that the little troupe could walk back to the train station faster than the traffic.

The highlight of the trip was the day at Wrigley Field. Uncle Joel's company had a block of season tickets and he had reserved these first base line tickets a long time ago just for the kids.

When Jason stepped into the stadium, felt the atmosphere and thought of its history, he almost lost his breath.

The organ music, crowd noises, echoes, ivy vines on the outfield walls, and the ground keepers putting the final touches on the field, made him weak in the knees. To see the Cubs take a game from the St. Louis Cardinals, just made the week complete.

After the game he heard a lot of popping noises. "What's that noise?"

"Just a bunch of dumb kids stomping on paper cups." Jessica said.

One final sight to see was Waveland Avenue and the little fire station he always heard so much about. He had to buy a Cubs cap from one of the vendors on the sidewalk, outside the stadium.

For years his dad had been talking to him about a day at Wrigley, but like so many other dreams and promises it never came. At times throughout the day Jason thought of what it might have been like with his dad at his side. But he was coming to see that life was rebuilding around him without his dad.

The week flew by, and as Jason got back on the train for home, he told his cousins, "Come down to Prairie Heights some time – that is, if you want to get a thrill watching corn grow!"

When he got home he spent the next few days bending the ears of his mother and his neighbors the Carlsons about the adventures in Chicago, claiming that he was going to live there someday.

It seemed that they took it all in like a good mom and neighbors; clearly thankful that he had a good time. Life in Prairie Heights soon reclaimed its rightful place in his thinking. Watching that corn grow returned to the daily routine. Hearing the trains blasting their horns off in the distance, at the north end of town, Jason realized it sounded better than the noise of the big city. It wasn't so bad here after all.

When he woke up the following Thursday morning, he woke up to a new level and a new order in his soul. He rolled over and punched his pillow as always, but this time there was finality to the act. Not only time to get up, but time for this boy to go to work. *Find a job, Greene.*

His mom, Michelle, was reading a cook book when he slid into the kitchen again in his white socks. "Well, son, what's on your busy schedule today?"

"Mom, it's time I go to work. Enough of this kid stuff. It's time for ole Jay here to earn his keep. I think Dad would want me to."

"I'm proud of you, son. So where will you start looking? Lawns to mow?"

"No, Mom, the Dawg Hause, of course. 'Member Doug asked Chris and me a coupla months ago when we were there for Sunday dinner?"

"I do remember, but that will mean some weekends, and Chris' parents are pretty tough on this thing about working on Sundays."

"Yeah, I know, Mom, but don't you agree I've got to start some time – some place? Chris will have to do what he thinks is best."

Reaching up to him, she said, "I'm so proud of you, son." She put down the book. "Here, don't go until I fill you with your favorite blueberry pancakes. I can't send my guy off to work hungry."

"Okay, I'll be back in a minute. I see Mr. C. out there washing his car again. He'll need a new paint job before a new car, the way he keeps washing that thing."

Out the door, across the porch, a punch on his post, and jumping into the driveway he took the hose from John and finished rinsing the left side of the SUV as he told him about the decision to get a job.

"Sounds great, Jay. Remember though, Doug as a boss will be different than Doug the friend. You'll have to start calling him Mr. Hauseman."

"Yeah, but that's part of my job right now, isn't it? – growing up."

"Boy, you are some kind of kid." Rubbing Jason's head, "I'm glad you're my neighbor. Most kids your age are still sleeping."

"Can't help what other kids do, Mr. C. Deep down my gut is just telling me it's time to get a job. Gotta go. Mom's doing that blueberry pancake thing for me this morning."

As Jason bounded back up on his porch, John called after him, "Jason, any parent would be glad to have a son like you. You're a credit to your dad, and your mom."

Jason stopped midstride and turned around to look John Carlson in the face. "Thanks, Mr. C. I needed that."

Chapter Fifteen

With pancakes resting comfortably in his belly, Jason powered his bike over the asphalt of Orlin Park sub-division to Main Street, then north to the Dawg Hause.

Doug was hanging onto a mug of coffee when Jason entered and boldly said, "Well, you asked me to come see ya for a job, remember? Where do I start? At the cash register?"

"No, no, hold on, young stallion," Doug said laughing. "Come into the office."

A half hour later Jason had the job and Doug told him to be at the restaurant at six in the morning next Saturday. Standing hard on the pedals of his bike and straining the chain all the way home, the fast rushing air made him feel glad he was now among the employed. He did wonder what Doug meant when he said, "You do know you'll start at the bottom of the food chain."

The battery alarm clock, from football experience, woke Jason up on Saturday. He cleaned up, grabbed a couple of cold Pop Tarts, climbed on his bike and rode through the early morning mist to the Dawg Hause. A cook answered his pounding on the back door at five-thirty.

"You must be the new kid. Anxious to start are you?"

"I guess so. I didn't want to be late the first day."

"Well come in and get something to eat. That's what people do here. Sparky will be here any minute. She'll get you started."

The cook put two slices of bread in the toaster. When they popped up he stabbed a knife through both before they fell back into the toaster and gave them to Jason. "Put all the butter and jelly on them as you want. Doug wants his help to be happy."

"Sounds good so far," Jason said.

"Oh, by the way," the cook added, "it's Alice Sparks or Miss Sparks to you. She's been here longer than any of us. She's the self-anointed supervisor, head waitress, hostess, chief cook and bottle washer, as well as manager. She's all work. Her bark is worse than her bite. Somewhere in her, none of us have found it, is a touch of compassion. But don't cross her."

With only two bites into the second piece of toast, Alice's bitter cold, piercing voice, aimed at the cook, entered the kitchen before she did. When the swinging door swung, she suddenly shifted her tone. "You must be Jason Greene. Doug told me you'd be here today. Early – that's good. Keep it up."

Without taking a breath, she continued, "Today, just do what I tell you to do. Don't get in the way of the servers. And whatever you do, don't drink or eat in front of the customers. Start with the broom and dust pan. The front walk needs sweeping every day when you start, and the parking lot needs to be picked up. You'll find the dumpster in the back. Any questions?"

"No, Ma'am. I know how to sweep."

Jason noticed Alice's eyes were still on him as she turned her head away with, "I hope that wasn't a smart answer."

"No, ma'am, I'm sorry." Jason grabbed the closest broom and found the nearest door. *This must be the bottom of the food chain.*

At seven on the dot Doug arrived and saw Jason in the parking lot picking up some trash swirling around the edges. "I see the boss got you started," Doug said. "I don't know when she took over, but it works out well. Behind her back the other girls call her the queen bee. Get the idea?"

"Yes, sir. I think I'll be okay."

After the parking lot was cleaned, a few delivery trucks unloaded and shelves stocked, Doug gave him a short tour of the dumpster area. "A clean dumpster pit shows a clean restaurant. Everything that goes in these things is either in a box or bag. Health department inspectors are always trying to find something on me. They check the dumpster area first. I'll depend on you to keep me out of trouble. Can you do that for me?"

"I sure can, Mr. Hauseman."

"Oh, by the way, over there to the right, in the cold weather is a large pile of split logs for the fireplace, like that big chain of Granny's Porch restaurants. Keep the fire going and keep the fireplace clean. You're on your own."

Alice gave him a break and then told him to vacuum the dining room. "Don't get too close to the remaining guests. Let them eat in peace."

At three in the afternoon, Doug told Jason he could leave and be back tomorrow at the same time. That would be Sunday, and he wondered if he should object. He quickly realized he didn't live a legalistic Christian life, so a Sunday without church on some weekends wouldn't make him a bad guy. He knew Doug was aware of how church was important to him. *It won't always be like this.*

For the next two months of the summer, Jason faithfully

reported to work when asked to – sometimes early, sometimes later when he had to be part of the closing act. He was kept busy with clearing sidewalks, parking lots and restrooms. He unloaded trucks and stocked shelves along with the cleaning of kitchen fans, filters, grease pit, and picking up the dining room. Jason took on these lowly jobs with personal responsibility. Doug and Alice could depend on him, but the time came when he began to grow weary with the brooms and grease pit.

One day, while feeling down at the bottom of that food chain for so long, and in a daring and courageous mood, he asked Alice, "Miss Sparks, why am I still doing the crummy jobs around here? By now I thought I'd be a server or host, or maybe working in a nicer part of this place."

In what must have been that rare and uncomfortable moment of compassion, the cook spoke of that first day, and clearly belying her image, Alice invited him to join her in a back booth with a coke. "Jason, you've done a good job for us since you started. When some other person starts they'll have your 'crummy jobs' as you call it, and you'll move up."

"The food chain?"

"Right."

"But others have started since I have."

"And you've seen them leave too, for one reason or another. They were often late or just didn't do a good job."

"So I stay at the bottom?"

Jason could see Alice was desperately trying to be gentle in her own clumsy way. With her thin, bony, liver spotted hands she took one of his large clear brawny hands and patted it. For once, she looked straight into his dark, sparkling ebony eyes. "Your day will come, Jason, I can promise you that. You have the qualities Doug and I want. Remember, Doug started out just like you for the Steins. You don't remember the dumpy Dog House on old number 6. The floors were full of broken tiles, parking lot was gravel and mud, and the restrooms were just nasty. He stuck with it and was greatly rewarded – you know the story."

"Yeah, I do."

"Watch him today and you'll still see him sweep or shovel the walk at times, and pick up paper when he comes into the building. You'll even see him bus and wipe off tables. That's the kind of leader he is, and that's what makes this the great restaurant we work in. He has bigger plans for this place and you can be a part of them."

"Thank you, Miss Sparks. I guess I was just feeling sorry for myself."

Patting Jason's hand again she said, "Gosh, kid, I wish you were twenty years older."

"Huh?"

"Oh, never mind," Alice said in a defeated voice.

Chapter Sixteen

After the summer trip to Chicago and starting work at the Dawg Hause, Jason realized quickly that his sophomore year in high school was starting out with little fanfare or excitement. The early walk in the halls was just one level higher than what he suffered as a freshman, but the juniors and seniors were still in charge.

Now at fifteen, Jason learned to catch on to the church thing that started three years ago when his dad became a Christian. He accepted the fact that at only twelve years old at the time, it was difficult to give up a day of fun for the sake of going to church. But Pastor Larsen began to make more sense to his ears now that his dad was gone, and he'd had to grab onto life by himself. Jason discovered a new Pastor Larsen when he saw the personal and tender side of him on that day he and the officers came to his house with the news of his dad's death. He saw the same pain in his Pastor's heart that he and his mother felt.

Sunday school had been even more difficult to start at twelve. The other boys in the class had grown up in it. Having Chris Young, his close friend at school, in the same class helped. Jason saw in Chris how a regular guy at school could also be a Christian. John Vardeen, the teacher, was a sharp guy who clearly understood the five boys in his charge and did a lot with them in and out of the church setting. Baseball games, picnics, hikes and so on were all part of Vardeen's attempts to show the boys that the Christian life also had a fun and social side.

Now in his sophomore year in school, and sometimes working on Sunday, Mr. Vardeen would often drop in at the Dawg Hause and let Jason know he still cared for him, and didn't get on his case about missing a Sunday in church once in a while. Jason felt church and Sunday school were okay, and he could see how they were having a positive effect on his daily moves and thinking.

Jason was working under one of the tables one day, trying to level the feet to stop it from wobbling, when he heard Doug Hauseman come in, talking to Alice Sparks. He didn't mean to listen, but he was too embarrassed to come out. So he stayed put.

"Alice," he heard Doug say, "You know the wandering, lost and empty days I spent after the death of my mother. You also know when I dropped out of school I didn't have the chance to play football or any other activities the kids have today. I'd like you to schedule these kids around those extra things the best you can."

"Well, I'll try, but you know it gets tight sometimes." Alice sounded a little flustered.

"I know what you're saying, Alice, but business is good, and if we have some extra kids around here at times we can get more things cleaned and polished. If we're short, you and I can do some serving and busing."

Jason knew, from experience, those words were not the sweetest song to Alice's heart, but she sounded as though she knew what he meant. The Steins had helped Doug

Hauseman so much that he now wanted to help others.

Doug continued, "Especially Jason Greene. His father, Marc was a close friend to me. Tried to talk me into staying in school. I really want to see that kid go places. He's good in football."

A minute later the room was empty and Jason emerged cautiously from the under the table, his face red, glad he had stayed unseen. He understood how Doug's encouraging attitude made the Dawg Hause a good place to work, and the customers clearly sensed it – it just helped the restaurant keep growing.

Jason knew from other guys that being a football player on the sophomore team was the time a kid like him had to make a decision to go on with the sport or give it up. *Who, besides moms, come to a sophomore game anyway? They're just used as the opening act for the varsity.*

He told Chris, Shawn, and Travis that this was their year of decision. One evening as they huddled in their favorite booth at the Dawg Hause, they made that decision. With all eight hands in a tight fist, they dedicated themselves to be the most aggressive and the greatest defensive front four players Prairie Heights and the conference ever knew.

"We'll listen to the coaches and do what they say, but we'll add our own touch to the moves," Travis said.

Chris added, "We'll get through any offensive line before they know what hit 'em"

"Let's hesitate, twist, twirl —" Jason said, but was cut off again by Travis.

"Side step and fake them out. No quarterback will be safe. Shawn, what are you going to add?"

"Well, if I could get a word in I would, but I can't add anything to all that. I'm in though. Instead of the usual trash talk on the line, we'll crack them up with new and great jokes. We can find out funny things about other kids at their schools. Let's add our own ideas to what the coaches tell us."

These growing hulks did just what they promised themselves they would. Halfway through the season the coaches caught on to what they had in those four. They threatened the senior team to notice what these guys were doing, or there would be fresh meat on the varsity line.

When Travis was asked to go onto the varsity team, the other three all asked, begged, the coaches not to break them up. The coaches were not overjoyed taking advice from sophomores, but reluctantly agreed that they were looking forward to the next two years.

The fearsome foursome, as they became known, tried to clue the varsity line in on some of their moves, but no one could pick up their panache. They won games by simply wearing down the other teams and quarterbacks. Their energy was kept alive with the fun they were having outfoxing the other teams with their audible laughter, jokes and snickering just before the ball was snapped; pulling countless players offside.

The coaches scratched their heads wondering what they were doing. On more than one occasion in each game they took the rule book to the edge – sometimes beyond – behind the backs of the referees. Radio announcers and reporters often made reference to the smiles they saw coming out of their helmets.

Back at the Dawg Hause one of Jason's first jobs when he got off the bottom of the food chain was squeezer of oranges. Saturdays and Sundays were wild with customers standing in long lines for their chance at the buffet or the belly buster breakfasts the Dawg Hause was famous for. Doug had many cases of oranges stacked in an area near the front door where Jason, or some other kid, did nothing but slice oranges and put them on the spinning tops of two industrial juicers. Pure filtered OJ poured out of the faucets, filling an unending line of large pitchers.

The seeds and pulp were strained out and discarded in large garbage containers. One day a man asked Jason if he could have a glass of just the pulp. "You're just going to throw it away anyway, right"?

"Yep. That's what I'm supposed to do." Jason caught Doug's eye and called him over to the stranger.

"Mr. H., this man would like a tall glass of just pulp. Can I give him one?"

Tilting his head in thought, Doug said. "I guess so. Can you keep the seeds out?"

"I'll do it."

With that first glass of pure pulp, given free to the stranger, came the idea that soon went on the menu as a glass of Pure Pulp. With a soda spoon and a two dollar price tag, Doug and Jason created a new product and more income for the restaurant from what used to be garbage.

After the orange juice incident, Doug told Jason he was now firmly on the Dawg Hause team, and it was time to raise him another level to a server, and let him really earn his keep.

Training started the next week. Alice was eager to get her hands into Jason as a server, where she could watch him more of the time. She laid it out plainly. "Our goal here is to out-service any other restaurant in town with a good attitude and personal attention. Keep on the go in busy time. No eating, drinking water, or personal conversation in front of the customers. Help each other and grab dirty dishes on your way to the kitchen. Remember the in and out doors –

think! Never handle glasses by the rim and always smile. No matter how grumpy a customer gets, be kind and help them. Bear in mind that the reputation of all of us and the Dawg Hause is at stake with your attitude. Take your aggression out on each other after the shift. When busing tables and booths, use the white cloth for wiping the eating areas and the blue cloth for the seats and benches."

Jason bought into all this and felt he honestly enjoyed working with the people who came into the restaurant – travelers as well as natives of Prairie Heights. Sometimes he wanted to laugh at the special touches customers requested. Like sour cream on the strawberry pancakes instead of whipped cream, no ice in the drinks, and "Tell the cook to really fry the hash browns to a cinder." He added his own flare and pampering to the service with a wink at times – especially to the old ladies, knowing it influenced the tips.

While walking home from school on a practice-less Monday, JT caught up to Jason and the secret duo got talking about sophomore stuff.

"I hear you and the guys are good in football," JT said.

"Yeah, it's going good. I'm glad Chris, Shawn, Travis, and I got that thing going."

"You guys are almost famous."

"I don't know about that. We're having fun though, thinking up new ideas."

JT took out a cigarette and lighting up, offered Jason one.

"Oh no. Remember what happened last time you took me there?"

"Yeah," JT said laughing. "You smoked your first and last butt that day. You're kinda smart, Greene. Smoking ain't all it's cracked up to be."

"Hey, if you're going to smoke I'm getting to the other side of you."

"How come?"

"So your smoke goes the other way with the wind."

"Now you're being stupid. Smoke don't make no difference. For some reason, though, I like you. You're okay. Hey, can I get a job at the Dawg Hause like you? A lot of kids work there, doesn't they?"

"Yeah, they do. I'll ask Mr. H. He demands a lot of work out of his people, and all new kids start at the bottom of the food chain."

"Huh?"

"You'll find out if you get the job. I'll ask him?"

"Hey, want to come up to the apartment? I got some great new triple-X rated movies."

Jason shook his head. He had reached his home now, and it was a good time for him to say, "No."

Chapter Seventeen

A Visit to Zig Ziglar
(Used by personal permission)

Jason gave his traditional two loud thumps on the back porch to signal to his mom that he was about to burst into the house. A split second later he flung open the door to the kitchen and it banged against the counter. In excitement he yelled, "Guess what, Mom. I'm going to hear Zig Ziglar! He's the guy Dad told us about a bunch of times, isn't he?"

"Easy son, I'd like to keep that door where it belongs. Now close it properly."

"Okay, but isn't Zig Ziglar the guy Dad said was a motivational speaker? What's that?"

"A motivational speaker motivates people."

"Yeah, I know that, but what does it mean?"

"Oh, my dear son. To motivate someone means to get them excited to do things – like do a better job, get a better job, keep a better job, to get along with people, clean your room, and other things – to succeed well in life."

"How can a guy do that just by *talking*?"

"Like you said when you ran in here; go hear him. By the way, how is all this going to happen?"

"Coach said Zig Ziglar is going to be at a big hotel in Peoria this Thursday, and he'd like to take the whole football team to hear him. Even some of us sophomores – he really wants us four to go. And get this – no practice that night."

"Wow, that must be important. I'm glad you'll get to see and hear him."

"Why do you say that?"

"Before your dad died in that helicopter crash he heard Zig Ziglar twice, and both times he came home almost as excited as you are now. But he didn't abuse my kitchen counter. He said his teaching and his time in the National Guard went better when he used that 'Zig stuff' as he called it."

Jason found it hard to get to sleep that night, and several times over the next two days at least two teachers nailed him for not paying attention in classes. On Thursday, as soon as school was over, most of the football teams and the coaches climbed aboard a big red charter bus from Peoria.

"No yellow school bus for this trip," the coach told them.

Riding on "Big Red" as the boys called it, was a thrill in itself. Reclining in the seats, using the foot rest, and adjusting the stream of fresh air onto their faces put them all in a good mood for a special evening.

When they arrived at the Great Room of the hotel, Jason hung back for a moment as they entered the massive place to the sound of up-beat music, a slightly hazy atmosphere and roving spotlight beams. He felt an electrifying expectancy throughout the entire room. The team followed the coaches to an area near the front, off to the left of the platform.

Within a few minutes the president of the local Chamber of Commerce bounded up to the platform, picked up the microphone and greeted the thousand plus people sitting in the chairs and standing around the edge of the room. After a few announcements and some lame jokes, he said, "Now let's put our hands together for a real 'Heart of Illinois' welcome for our favorite Texan, *Zig Ziglar!*"

The room erupted into applause, whistles, cheers, and yelling. Jason wondered why all this hype for just a guy who's going to talk. *This might be better than a sermon.* He didn't even see a speaker on the platform.

A yell of, "*Howdee ...*" from the rear of the room was followed by a man in a blue suit running down the aisle, and in a single leap he was on the platform shaking hands with the announcer.

With the microphone firmly gripped in his hand, Zig said, "Thank you, thank you, thank you. It's great to be back here again. What I remember about Peoria is the last time I was here the stage collapsed under me. Nobody was hurt, but it sure woke 'em up. Another way I keep them alert is like the cross-eyed javelin thrower. He didn't score much, but he sure kept the folks in the stands awake.

"I'd like to tell you another little story. A few months ago a young reporter interviewed me when I came to do a series of presentations in his town. He said, 'You come a long way to talk to these folks, don't you?'

"Yep, I said."

"You get a lot of money for doing this, don't you?"

"I guess you could say that."

"You try to motivate these people, don't you?"

"That's right, I hope to."

"So you think motivation is permanent then, don't you?"

"When I said no, he was really confused."

"If it isn't permanent, why do you talk about it all the time?"

"I couldn't help this, so I clued him in. 'No, motivation's not permanent, but neither is deodorant.' He was blown away with this. He looked like I'd hit him with a brick. I thought I'd better explain it for the kid. You see for deodorant to be effective, you have to keep putting it on every day. Motivation is like that too. To be effective you have to keep putting it on. We're going to learn how to do that, right here – tonight.

"Now, I'm not a pharmacist, but I am going to give you some vitaminds. I call them vitaminds – vitaminds for your mind, of course. Like this one. 'You can have everything in life you want – if you will just help enough other people get what they want.' Or, 'When you help someone else to the mountaintop, you get there too.'

"Before I go on any further, I see a lot of young people here tonight including this group to my right. Where are ya'll from?"

In unison, several of the guys yelled, "Prairie Heights football teams."

"Fantastic! Great! What we're going to be talking about tonight is just as important to you as it is to all the businessmen or women here. Okay, time for me to go to work.

"It's a big crowd here, but from the noise I've heard so far I'm sure you can all participate properly in the potential presentation. Answer this question with one word. Shout it out to me. What qualities or characteristics do you respect and admire in successful people you know? Get that? What is it successful people have that you look up to and admire? I'll jot them down here on the overhead so you can keep a running idea of them – and write them down. Go ahead now, yell them out."

Jason sat transfixed as words were shouted from all over

the room. Some members of the P.H.H.S. football team raised their hands like they would in school, but quickly caught on that this circus put them in another ballgame. Zig wrote them down on the overhead as fast as he could, raising his hand once in a while to slow the crowd down and make a comment.

Honest, outgoing, considerate, goal setter, were some of the first words called out.

Suddenly Zig stopped the shouting. "Listen, give me a stock clerk with a goal, and I will give you a man who will make history. Give me a man without a goal, and I will give you a stock clerk. J.C. Penney said that a long time ago. You know who worked for J.C. Penney? A guy with the name of Sam Walton, the founder of Walmart. Look where he went. This goal-setting business is more important than a lot of people realize. Let me ask this football team a question. What's the main thing you want to do in a game?"

Jason jumped as his chunky friend Chris yelled out, "Score points."

"And how do you do that?" Zig asked.

"Cross the goal line, of course," Chris called back, as he laughed and looked at his friends.

"Bingo!" Zig said with a big smile. "See what I mean? If it's so important to reach a goal in a football game, or any game, how much more important is it to reach your goals in life? Let's have some more."

Morality, patience, initiative, sincerity, leadership, good choices, being happy.

"Wow, there's a good one I haven't thought of. Did you know that being happy is a choice? You can be miserable by choice too. It's up to you."

By the sound of the enthusiasm it seemed to Jason they were just getting started.

Persistence, consistent, enthusiastic, dependable.
"Whoa, whoa, partners. This pen can only go so fast. You're good. I hope you see where this is going. It's the dependable people that are asked to do the big jobs. They're the people who get things done." Looking to his right at the football team, he said, "And that goes for sports too. Remember, 'There's no I in team.' Let's keep going."

No I in team; heard that before. Jason looked around at the other players. It seemed that most of them remembered what Coach told them on the first day. They looked over at the coach smiling, and as he looked back at them he pointed to Zig and nodded his head.

Courageous, extra effort, humble, well dressed, organized, firm, good attitude.

At this point Zig fell to his knees, threw up his hands, and let the pen fly loose into the crowd. "That's the magic word tonight. Attitude is everything. If I could, I'd chisel 'attitude' into every heart. More about that later. Keep them coming."

Helpful, mature, generous, sense of humor, integrity, character, confident, on time.

"Stop! Whew, you folks don't slow down, do you? *On time.* I don't know where this generation gets the idea that the time thing isn't important. This great country, with its economy, industry, growth, military, sports, and progress, has been achieved by people working together and being on time.

"Folks, your bosses may not tell you eyeball to eyeball, but they know who's late or on time – always."

Zig asked supervisors, managers, and CEOs of companies to stand up. "Raise your hands if you know who the late ones are in your business."

To a person, all raised their hands.

"I guess I don't have to say much more about that. Just who do you think he or she will promote when the opportunity comes up? Hmmm? Don't stop now. We've only just started."

Dedicated, self-confident, responsible, caring, intelligent, risk taker, compliment others.

"Right, hey, get this. A sincere compliment is one of the most effective tools to teach and motivate others. Hear that, coaches? Give me one more."

Someone yelled, "They like Mondays."

Stepping back, throwing his arms up and letting the pen fly into the audience again, Zig said, "Wow, talk about hitting the nail on the head. Who said that?"

He couldn't find the person in that big crowd, but as he thumped his finger on the word, *Monday*, he went on to say, "Think about this. We all know what T.G.I.F. means. How many of you can say, T.G.I.M. and mean it? A lot of people don't have a job to go to on Monday. A lot of people can't go to school on Monday. Many can't get out of *bed* on Mondays. Some have no opportunities to do anything on Mondays, or they fight Mondays like a disease. Listen to ole Zig now, kids."

Calling the audience of adults, kids, brought a lot of laughter.

"If you can conquer Monday mornings, you'll conquer the week and be light years ahead of the competition. God bless the one who said that. I'll hire you right now – I'll find some job for you. Got some more? I bet you do."

Decision maker, good listener, creative, energetic, straightforward, determined, good self-esteem, encourager.

Jason hung his head and quietly thought, *Dad, Dad, Dad,* as he heard Zig continue.

"Hold up a minute here again. This pen is starting to smoke. Look at the last two qualities. Good self esteem and encourager. Think how these two go together. If you don't care much for yourself, how can you help someone else? See, another vitamind. Many people have gone farther than they thought they could because someone *else* thought they could. Think about that one – one more time."

The words started to come slower now, but there still was a steady stream. *Committed, hard worker, attentive, open minded, friendly, communicator.*

"Let's stop here. This could go on for a long time and there is a lot to be said about each word, but the point has been made. You'll also note that the last words are as important as the first. I hope you've copied this list.

"Before we go any farther, I'd like to define two words we'll work with now. A skill is a developed talent or ability you achieve by training and practice. Like playing a piano, plumbing, dentistry, or driving a truck.

"Attitude is an inner characteristic that is expressed by an action or way of thinking. Now, when I point to each of these words, tell me if it's an attitude or skill."

As Zig touched one word after another the audience yelled out, "Attitude" or "Skill." Sometimes both words were shouted. Jason sat with his friends in their seats amused by watching all these adults so involved and excited over this little game.

As the team looked around at what sounded like an auction, they began to hear the word Attitude being called out much more than the word Skill. The coaches were all caught up in this. Jason could see that men and women around him were all excited, and even Zig Ziglar was having fun.

"Remember the question we started with? What do you

respect and admire in successful people you know? Every group of people I talk to call out the same list. Conventions of dentists, union leaders, teachers, city workers, funeral directors, or any crowd; by a large majority you have agreed with them. It is Attitudes."

He stepped back, folded his arms and just grinned.

"You've just agreed that these words describe successful people."

Leaning towards the audience and with a quiet emphasis he said, "Do they describe *you?*

"Now if all this has some of you worried, the best news is yet to come."

Kneeling on one knee and pointing to the P.H. football team, "You young people," then swinging his arm in a wide ark to include the entire audience, "every one of you can develop these attitudes into your life like you develop skills. Look, if you want more honesty in your life – practice it. Want more initiative – work on it. Want to beat the Monday morning blues – get up. More leadership, more intelligence? Take some classes and learn. Want to be early or on time more often?" He came right to the edge of the platform, leaned over the crowd again and said, with open hands, "Just do it! Impose your own starting time ten minutes earlier.

"Friends, we all know the wisdom of the ages is, 'There ain't no free lunch.'" Tapping his finger on the words again, he said, "The successful people you respect and admire have worked and developed these characteristics to a fine skill, and they use them every day. The end of the matter is, you can be there too. People can look at you and see this list.

"Hey, while we're on this subject, there is a new movement in our culture that is making it difficult for these good attitudes to exist. *It's all about me* is growing like a cancer.

No one would admit it though. It usually comes out as *It's all about you*, doesn't it?' It shows up in selfishness, tardiness, laziness, snide and sarcastic remarks. Not only do employers, family, and friends dislike this characteristic, it will absolutely paralyze a person in their drive to be successful."

When Zig made that statement, Jason looked around in awe as hundreds of people jumped to their feet and applauded wildly.

"I can't help but point this out to our young people here tonight. Kids, do you see who is doing all the applauding? Old folks, fifty-five or over who have learned this the hard way. I want you to know, you will believe this list we have made. You'll either believe it now and put it to use in your life, or you'll discover it when you're fifty-five or older when it's too late. But you will learn it."

More wild applause. The last words of Zig's presentation were, "You folks do these things just as you said here, and I truly will, '*See You At The Top*.'"

Jason couldn't believe his ears when the audience really came alive with applause, whistles, and more cheers. He could sense that the football team was amazed at the excitement and energy everyone had even after more than two hours. This must be motivation.

When Zig Ziglar finished his presentation he thanked the audience for their enthusiasm by saying, "You guys did all the work. I'll stick around and meet as many of you who want to say 'Hi,' but I want to meet this football team first so they can get back home, if that's okay with ya'll."

He came off the platform to the coaches, shook their hands and congratulated them for bringing the boys to a meeting like this. He started to shake hands with each of the team, and when he came to Jason, Jason told him, "My dad heard you speak a coupla times, and now I know why he always talked about you."

"Your dad is one of the coaches here?"

"No, sir, my dad died a coupla years ago in a helicopter crash."

"Your dad in the military?"

"Yep, the National Guard."

"He died while serving his country, did he?"

"Yes, sir, he did."

Zig grabbed Jason's head and held him close to his chest, unashamedly. "I'm so sorry, son, but I want you to know that I personally thank you for the sacrifice you and your mom have made for our country."

"Thank you, Mr. Ziglar. I'll tell her."

"You do that. Thanks again and God bless you."

The kitchen counter took another beating when Jason got home.

"Jay, that door!"

"Sorry, Mom. Boy what a great night. I see why Dad talked so much about Zig Ziglar. I picked up as much free stuff as I could off the tables and I'd like to get his book. Coach said he'd try and get some copies for us. I even took notes on some paper I found."

"I'm impressed. You must have had a good time."

"Yeah, even the bus driver, Ken Unisses – Unes, or something like that – he was cool."

"Son, it's after midnight and you've got school tomorrow. Please go to bed."

"Yeah, Coach told us even though it's late, don't miss school tomorrow. Mom, I'll go to bed, but I can't sleep. I'm really wired. I just met Zig Ziglar!"

Chapter Eighteen

After the euphoria of seeing and hearing Zig Ziglar, the rest of the sophomore year seemed a little dull. Jason began to wake up to the movements of life around him. Rushing in crowded hallways between classes became an exercise in timing and twisting, just like football. Teachers were always standing guard in the heat of passing time, ever since a "concerned" mother complained that her little girl was "trampled on."

Jason tried to keep a clean and organized locker, but with little success. Stopping one morning to say "Hi," to JT, he noticed all sorts of debris falling out of JT's locker. "How can you live like that?"

"Hey, it's my house. I'm good with it."

"How do you find stuff in there?"

"There ya go again – being the cop." Opening the locker wider so JT could stuff more torn books back in, Jason noticed the wallpaper on the back of the door, and his eyelids went up like a cartoon cat finding a mouse. "Those pictures! The girls don't have any clothes on."

"Well daugh, shut up, Greene, it's my life."

"What if someone sees 'em?"

"You kidding? Who ever looks into JT's locker? Who

even *talks* to me? No one cares about me or my stupid locker."

An envelope fell on the floor without JT noticing. Jason picked it up and saw it was addressed to Joseph – couldn't make out the last name. He handed it to JT and said quietly, "Your name is Joseph?"

Hearing "Joseph," JT twisted his head around so fast his neck snapped. "Gimmie that." He whipped it out of Jason's hand, took a handful of his T-shirt in his other fist and stuck his face so close to Jason's their noses collided. "You never saw that, Greene."

Feeling his life was threatened all by this sudden hostility, Jason knew he got the message.

"Okay, Greene, so you know what my first name is, but don't ever say it out loud where others can hear it. That's another secret you and I have. Got that?"

"Loud and clear, JT. Don't worry, I'll guard it with my life."

Using the language of a drunken sailor, JT said, "You got that right – with your life."

Because of the confrontation at JT's locker, Jason arrived at Mr. Melbourne's Social Studies class five or seven seconds late. Mr. Melbourne was the worst teacher in the school with this "on time" thing, but today he was opening a window as Jason came through the door. Jason took advantage of his good fortune and quickly slipped into his desk. The snickering of some of the students over this transgression did not go unnoticed by Mr. Melbourne.

He swung around with, "What's going on?"

Seeing half the class looking at the ceiling with stupid looks on their faces, he obviously knew he'd get no answer, so he started class.

After a dry bones lecture on exploration, Mr. Melbourne

passed out the test he'd told them yesterday was coming. While taking the test, Jason noticed a few of the answers were still on the white board at the front of the room. His eyes shifted side to side to see if anyone else noticed them.

As Jason passed by Mr. Melbourne's desk on the way out of the room, he leaned over and whispered. "Did you know you left some of the answers on the board?"

"Do say? Did you make use of the opportunity?"

"Yes, sir, I did," Jason said quietly.

"Remember this, Mr. Greene. To the observant belong the solutions. I leave three to four answers up there for the observant like you. It amazes me how many kids don't even notice. Good luck, have a good lunch."

In the second semester of Jason's sophomore year he began to feel he had found his place in school and in the town. Working at the Dawg Hause put him into the public eye. He heard how more and more people in town came to appreciate "Marc and Michelle's kid" as he carved out a productive and independent life, in spite of the great loss of his dad.

Pole vaulting was going exceptionally well. During an invitational meet at another school Jason noticed a photographer taking pictures, mostly of the pole vaulters. At one time the photographer set his camera up right next to the pocket where the jumpers jammed the pole. The view was straight up the pole as he crossed over the bar ten feet above. Jason received a copy of the picture and Coach Towers had it blown up to poster size where it ended up on the gym wall. Jason knew it was a great tribute and honor, to say nothing about the ego it fed him. It later found its final resting place on the back of the door in his room at home.

* * *

Driver's Education was next on Jason's plate and if anyone was ready to hang up bike, skateboard, and rollerblades, it was Jason Marc Greene. Even Michelle and his neighbors the Carlsons said they were happy for him because it meant less or no carting him to practice after practice in sports and dozens of other events. Especially the emergency runs to the Dawg Hause could be made by himself if he was running late. He didn't want the wrath of Alice grinding on him for the day.

Jason was glad that he had his favorite PE teacher and coach, Mr. Dole, as the driving instructor, and he knew this was an added benefit to him. He took on this class with a passion and did very well. Even the classroom part of the experience was exciting.

Mr. Dole dragged on and on with the same sage advice, stories, and lessons he'd given for years. "You're going to be driving the rest of your lives, so do it right. Start collecting tickets and insurance claims and you'll be in for a long, expensive, and troublesome trip. I know drivers who haven't had a ticket or even a simple accident for thirty years or more – not even a parking ticket."

He pointed to each face. "But you'll all have to learn the hard way. From what I know of those who have gone before you, you'll all have some scrape of one kind or another within two years of this class, maybe within just one. I read the paper and my wife hears me say, 'I told you so' all the time."

Jason vowed within himself, *Not I, Dole. Keep reading all you want.*

When it came time for behind-the-wheel driving, Jason came to the event with another secret he was holding close to his chest. For over a year, John Carlson had taken Jason out on the far back roads of Prairie Heights. Up and down hills, curves and sharp turns; backing up and parking; even driving in the snow and ice. Once he borrowed an older car with stick shift and showed Jason the art of clutch.

Mr. Dole could tell Jason had some kind of advantage. Chris Young, Jason's best friend was too serious, Shawn McClintock was too skittish, and Travis Valdez was too aggressive for a beginner. Dole was always telling – yelling – at him to slow down. Sharon Warwick, the girl whom Jason was watching closer and closer from time to time with growing interest, was just plain scared with every move. When she was driving, the ones in the rear seat just slouched, and tried to be quiet.

One day when returning to the school and getting out of the car, Mr. Dole quietly asked Jason privately, "You've been driving before somewhere, haven't you?"

"Yeah, I have."

"Don't tell me anything more, Mr. Greene."

At the end of the school year Jason completed his "sentence" with a driver's permit and flunked the driver's test the first time. After the second try and passing it, at a back porch barbecue with the Carlsons in celebration of the event, he let off some steam. "I know more about driving than all the other kids put together. The examiners just had it in for me."

"Son," his mom said quietly, "most kids don't make it on their first try."

"Yeah, but I've had more experience than most of the guys."

"Maybe that's my fault, Jay," John Carlson said. "Maybe we drove too much and the examiner thought you were too confident. He had to take some of the wind out of your sails."

Rubbing Jason's head, Karen Carlson said, "Don't go to war over this issue. We're glad you can drive, and we know you'll be a good driver."

Doug gave JT a job and became the only man in town, other than the school superintendent, to know what JT's last name was – because he needed it for Social Security reasons. Still the application and pay checks read only JT. Working at the Dawg Hause didn't work for JT. He was late most of the time and argued with Alice and Doug.

"I think Doug saw himself in JT and was hoping things would work out, but his work was sloppy," Alice told Jason. "So we had to let him go. He even seemed relieved when I told him."

"I guess I can understand that, Miss Sparks."

"Tell me something, Jason. Why is it that you seem to be his only friend in town? Everyone else stays away from him like the plague."

"JT and I talked about that one day about a year ago and we discovered we have something in common."

"Now just what in the *world* would Jason Greene and JT have in common?" Alice said, in her pushy and demanding way.

"No dad, Miss Sparks. No dad. We've got a connection there. We do get along – if I don't get too close."

"Make sure you don't."

While Jason went about his work at the restaurant, he spoke to many people from Prairie Heights. He guessed he was well liked as some of them would drop a bill or two in his busing tub or put some money in his shirt pocket. He thought the older ladies in town used the brief touch to his chest as their thrill of the day. A quick peck on his dimpled cheek seemed to put them into orbit and a return visit soon.

"That's for making your dad proud," they would say.

Once Alice told him that she never saw a kid get so many tips. "You must lead a charmed life."

"Miss Sparks, you know my life isn't all charmed."

That summer, Doug Hauseman told his staff he was determined to remodel and add on to the restaurant. Off to the side with a separate classy entrance, he built the "Stein Banquet Hall." He made it the best designed and appointed formal dining room in town. He turned over the new design for the front entrance to the Dawg Hause to his high school employees. A move that almost became his undoing.

When the kids were done, there was a front door that looked like the door of a dog house, complete with clapboard siding and a child's painted sign, "Spot," hanging over the entrance – crooked. A large sign in the yard said, "Beware of the dawg." It had a dog's bite out of a corner. For a stake in the ground they used a leaning telephone pole with a five foot logging chain leading from it – broken.

Inside the restaurant, booths were named after the breeds of dogs such as Boxer, Doberman, Collie, Poodle, and the like. The tables were names of famous dogs like Lassie, Rin-Tin-Tin (always a question Who?), Bullet, Fido, Rover, Snoopy etcetera. Repeat customers had their favorites, and even waited for them to open up.

It wasn't long before the front lawn of the restaurant was the setting for senior portraits and family pictures. Doug and his kids, "the Dawg Hause Gang," continued to prosper. It made exit 56 on Interstate 80 famous. At the same time as the remodeling and addition of the banquet hall, the Dawg Hause Gang changed the menu to include a Friday night "Fry Fest." It consisted of five different styles and shapes of

French fries. Not a great item for adults, but kids went for it in a big way.

Another trip to Chicago that summer convinced Jason more than ever that he just had to live in that city, at least for some part of his life. His cousin Keith now had a car of his own and when Jason returned to Prairie Heights his head was full of buying a pickup.

Chapter Nineteen

A few days back home and thinking about Keith's car, Jason figured out it was okay for Keith to have a car in Wheaton, but in Prairie Heights, a guy has got to have a pickup. "There's a nice bunch of pickups at all the dealerships in town. They come in all colors too." Jason dropped half dozen brochures on the table in front of John Carlson. "Look, they've got coil-over shock front suspension, hydro form technology, dual glove box storage, heated mirrors and seats and lots of other stuff. Which one would you buy?"

"None."

"Huh?"

"Friend, what are you going to do with your pickup? Carry heavy loads, plow snow, drag, go off road, drive it in parades, climb mountains? Don't see any of them in Illinois do you?"

"No, I just want to get around town in class."

"Ever think of used?"

"No! Keith got a new car in Wheaton."

"What's your income, Jay?"

"About a hundred to a hundred thirty bucks a week – that includes tips."

Jason saw John bite his lip to keep from laughing. "Son,

with payments, insurance, license, gas, and fast food, you could go well over a thousand dollars a month. What's your income again?"

"Well, how's a kid suppose to get a car?"

"Start at the bottom, Jay, just like the rest of us."

"Oh, bottom of the food chain thing again, huh?"

"Yep. You don't think I started with that Escalade out there did you? You see pictures of your dad and mom when they were dating? What kind of cars were in the pictures?"

"Dorkey, big old things with rust holes in the fenders."

"I rest my case. My first car was a Rollscanardly."

"I never heard of that one."

"It's a car that rolls down one hill and can 'ardly make it up the next. If I wanted to impress a date, I'd have to ask dad to use his car. Your mom would let you use her Buick, and if you really wanted to blow some pretty young thing's mind you could borrow my SUV."

"Wow! Can I?"

"Not today, Jay."

"All that money stuff. Where do all the kids at school get their new cars? Got dads? Blake has a new car, but look where his dad works."

"Easy, friend, don't go there. That could well be the case, but look deeper into yourself. If I know anything about your father, he would want you to make it on your own: like he did. He left you with good common sense to work through conflicts, and a gift for thinking things out. Few guys have that kind of foundation."

Jason nodded slowly. After four years, echoes and visions of the canoe trip and his dad's words still paraded through his mind. Suddenly his consciousness left John Carlson, and in a moment of reflection he was at the fire with his dad at Frosty Point. *"You'll always have struggles in life, son. Things will not always be fun and games like they are today. Think first. Hold your tongue. Stand on solid ground. You'll not always have all the answers – no one does. Just because you'll find yourself in conflict at times, doesn't mean you have to like it. See it through – deal with it. Situations change, son. It won't always be like it is at the time."*

"Jay, where are you?" Mr. Carlson's voice brought Jason back to the discussion of a pickup.

"Not a new pickup, huh?"

"Not this time, but don't give up. What do you think John Vardeen your Sunday school teacher would tell you to do?"

"He'd tell me to pray about it. Hey! That's what Dad would do too, wouldn't he?"

"You do catch on quick, Jay"

For the next three weeks, while sneaking to work on his bike or skateboard through back alleys, Jason griped about his wheel situation to everyone from JT to Doug Hauseman.

JT laughed in his face. "Greene, you can't lose. Something will turn up. Be glad you're not me. I don't stand a chance with a car. I still don't have a license. Who'd let me use their car to even *take* the stupid test? Would your mom let me use her Buick?"

"But you've got your motorcycle." Suddenly realizing a motorcycle required a license. Jason quickly added, "No license?"

"Oh, that old thing. It barely runs. Funny thing, as much as the cops hate me in this town, they leave me alone and let me get around on it."

When the doors opened for school in his junior year, Jason was one busy kid with football, homework, working at the restaurant, car hunting, and the social calendar where Sharon Warwick began to take up time. When the football practice issue came around that year, Alice reluctantly carried out Doug's request of scheduling his work at the Dawg Hause around practices and games. He worked as much as he could even on some Sundays. Chris Young's dad really put his foot down and told him, "No Sunday work." It worked for a while, but Chris could see the hardship on Alice and others, so he got another job.

As a junior and a more muscular machine on the football field, Jason pushed, hit, tackled, and simply banged into other players more than before. He still found the aggressive action an outlet for much of his reserved reputation.

The fearsome four from P.H.H.S. defensive line practiced more than ever to keep the edge on their now famous moves. They even practiced in Shawn's solid wooden fenced-in back yard so no spies could see them. The coaches were always amazed what they would come up with, without breaking the rules. The referees soon got their number, and other things in the games went unnoticed as they watched the four for any cheating. This even gave the other players of Prairie Heights time to try some unsavory tricks.

Since freshman year, Sharon had her hooks bated for Jason. She was a firecracker of a girl and kept mild mannered Jason off his balance. In their morning walks before school, now that the juniors were in control and they were at the hand-holding level, they discussed heavy subjects like, why did we get our names?

"Sometimes I wonder what my parents were thinking when they named me Sharon. I hate it. Why would anyone name a kid Sharon? It's so old fashioned. Why do parents do things like that?"

"Gee, I don't know. Something they had to do suddenly

one day I guess. I never thought of you as old fashioned."

Looking up into Jason's face, she said, "Really? You don't think so? What about you? You like your name?"

"I never thought about it much either. Yeah, I like the name Jason. I'm glad I also have my dad's name."

"What's that?"

"Marc."

"Mark! That's the coolest middle name I ever heard. Usually middle names are stupid."

"Dad was a cool guy. He spelled it M-A-R-C. But, of course, his folks did the naming, I guess."

"That's cooler yet. Talking about names," Sharon said, "I'm going on my own personal quest to find out what JT's name is. I'm working in the counseling office as an intern and I file lots of folders. I'm going to find out just what the 'J' and the 'T' stand for."

Their walking suddenly stopped as Jason squeezed her hand tightly. "Don't do it, Sharon," he said in a frightened and demanding voice. "Don't do it. For some reason he guards that information with his iron fists. My advice is, forget it and forget it fast. It's just JT. To all of us."

"Hey, don't freak out on me."

"Just a warning," Jason said. "I don't want you to get lost in the river with cement boots on."

They headed for different classes, Sharon looking completely befuddled.

Another new addition to the school that year was Dr. Cecil Barton. He blew into town from the Minneapolis school system and was different from any superintendent the kids ever knew. He'd be in the halls every morning talking to them in their language. "How 'bout them Cubbies?" And on Monday mornings he'd ask the guys, "What did you think of

'Da Bears'?" For the girls, he complimented them on their clothes and always had a silly joke for them. Like the one about the two cannibals eating a clown. "One said to the other, that taste funny to you?"

There was an immediate friendship between superintendent and students, but still the respectful distance.

Dr. Barton quickly learned of Jason's background and the fearsome four. He also caught a sampling of JT one morning when he became the first faculty member in history to stop by on one of his rounds before school and visit JT at his locker. "Well, young man, you have quite an art collection in your closet there."

"Yeah, ya like it? Want to take some out on loan?"

Chuckling, Dr. Barton said, "No, but when I need a calendar I'll know where to find one."

"Hey, you might be okay, Doc, I jus —"

"It's Dr. Barton to you, friend, just like all the others."

"Okay, I heard that. We'll get along."

Leaning close to JT's ear, Dr. Barton said, "It's my job to know about my students. If there is anything I can do for you, son, let me know."

JT's quick sensitive and perceptive nervous system understood that remark fully. Looking around back and forth over his shoulder like a used car salesman he said, "Our secret, sir?"

"Gotcha." With that fast but intimate introduction, the bell rang. Dr. Barton shook JT's hand, much to his surprise, and said, "Sounds like time for the boss to go to work."

One afternoon in the bank, Doug Hauseman and Matthew Blake, the father of Jason's friend Tim, the car dealer in town, crossed paths. Mr. Blake nudged Doug to a corner and spoke to him about a liquor license for the Dawg Hause.

"I was just talking to the mayor and he told me there's a liquor license available. I think you should grab it up; at least for the Stein part of your place."

Doug had this conversation before with other businessmen in town and his answer was always No. "Matt," Doug responded, "a long time ago I told myself I'll run my restaurant without liquor in any form. I have a good reputation to hold up and I don't want to give my kids any opportunity to the stuff. I don't want any of it in the store rooms."

"I can't see how your business can keep up these days without at least serving beer."

"It's been going and growing strong now for more than twenty years. How many other business owners in this town do you know who operate with no debt? I don't see the business going down."

"Hauseman, you've got your head in the sand. Liquor is where the money is."

"So are lawsuits, accidents, broken families, and a lot of other misery. I've got a good thing going and I see no reason to change it. I sleep very well and have a clear conscience every time I come into this bank – if you get my drift."

"You're making a big mistake, Doug. I could help you get that license."

With a hand on Matthew Blake's shoulder, Doug said, "I hear from the parents of my kids that they appreciate not having liquor in the restaurant. I couldn't buy that kind of support. Besides, I still see you and your family in there a lot. Thanks, but no thanks for the license."

"Doug, like I said, I think you're making a big mistake. But somewhere in my thinking I respect what you are doing at that restaurant. Wish I could run a business without debt."

Chapter Twenty

One day when Jason was helping the dishwasher sort out the crud from the crumbs at the restaurant, Doug Hauseman moved next to him. "I hear you're looking for some wheels."

"Yeah, you gonna give me your Hummer?"

"Not today, but I do have a great used pickup I just broke in eighteen years ago, and I think you'd fit right into it."

Turning his back on the dirty dishes, Jason and Doug walked to another corner of the kitchen. "I didn't know you had a pickup, Mr. H."

"I keep it locked up. Had it for all its eighteen years. It used to be my workhorse in the early days."

"What kind of condition is it in?"

"I've always kept it in good mechanical condition, but the body needs work. I thought of making it over, but I lost interest in it when the restaurant took off so well."

"When can I see it? Where is it? How much do you want for it? Got heated seats and all that new stuff?"

"I'll bring it by your house this evening about eight, and you and your crew can look it over. Remember, the body needs work. I don't want you to think you're going to be looking at a cherry."

Jason, with his homework done early, and Chris Young at his house, were waiting in the driveway at seven thirty. His mom Michelle and the Carlsons told Jason they hadn't seen him so pumped up for a long time. At eight on the dot, something resembling a pickup rattled up the driveway. Deflated as a flat tire, Jason said to John Carlson and Chris in a low voice, "Boy, it sounds old. It's just limping up the drive."

"Let's see what he's offering," John whispered back.

Like a group of vultures swarming over road kill, Michelle, Jason, Chris, and the Carlsons touched, rubbed, kicked, and did everything except take the pulse of the sputtering specimen, while Doug Hauseman kept reading their eyes.

"Here's the deal," Doug said. "Three hundred dollars. It works great. I've always had Mickey the mechanic keep it in good shape."

"Mickey! Greatest wrench in town," John said.

"Like I told you, the body needs work, but for the price, you can learn some bodywork and have all the wheels you want. It's not for life, you know," Doug said.

Jason and Chris walked to the other side of the truck whispering among themselves, and Jason could hear Doug say to his mom, "I could give the thing to Jason, but I think he should learn to pay something for..."

"Good idea, Doug," she answered. "He should pay something. Thanks."

On the other side of the truck, a spark went off in Jason's head. He elbowed Chris. "Follow my lead. I can do it. I can do it. I'll learn how to work with body putty..."

Chris interrupted with, "We can get Tim Blake to help

us. He knows bodywork."

"Yeah, yeah, and I'll paint it orange, just like Moose's truck."

"Orange!" yelled his mom. "Why orange? And who is this Moose guy?"

"The guy from the canoe place who picked us up at the Duluth airport. You remember him, don't you, Mr. C.?"

"Yeah, I do, but he painted his pickup orange because he drove it in the woods during hunting season. You don't need it orange in Prairie Heights."

"I think it will be cute," Karen said in a rare statement. Leaning close to Michelle, she added quietly, but overheard by Jason, "When the time comes, I'm sure he'll paint it something decent."

"Pay me fifty bucks a month," Doug said. "I'll be the banker. No Mr. Seymour Franklin and his bank in this deal. I won't take it out of your salary. You make the payments."

With a handshake, the deal was finalized. Jason and Chris gave Doug a ride home in the new acquired wheels with questionable use of the clutch.

"Where did you learn to drive a clutch, Jay?" Chris asked.

"Mr. C. borrowed an old car some time ago and he taught me that too."

When Jason returned from dropping Chris off at his place, the Carlsons and Michelle were on his back porch having some coffee. In his sometimes unwanted opinion, John Carlson said, "Registration, a license plate and insurance stand in your way from putting this beast on the streets. The extra expenses start now."

"Insurance on this thing?"

"Liability, yes. Collision, no. Know the difference, Jay?"

"Yep. Liability on other people I might hit, and collision

is for this crate. But I won't wreck it."

During the winter months, Jason and his friend Chris learned and applied their efforts to working on the body of the pickup in Jason's garage. Tim Blake helped a lot with the expertise he learned from working with the guys in his father's body shop at the car dealership. Getting the supplies wholesale also helped hone their craft.

For weeks the truck body, stripped from all its old and rusty dignity, showed only its naked frame. The three boys picked up a mechanic's feel of grease and paint, knuckles torn open by slipping wrenches, all mixed with late hours and talk of victory.

When he finished, Jason found out he could not afford a nice finish on the truck, so he hand brush painted it – green, of course. Not a soft green but more of a neon green. It became known as "Big Green." No question who was coming up the street at high noon – or even after dark. Jason felt that wherever it was parked, the population of Prairie Heights would know right where Jason Greene was.

In February of that year, Sharon Warwick told Jason that she'd been doing her usual filing of student folders for Mr. Johnson, one of the counselors, in the file room. She explained that the temptation to find out what that famous T stood for in JT got the best of her emotions. Mr. Johnson's student load was from A to H, but today, her fingers were walking in the T drawer.

From behind her, she heard Mr. Johnson's voice. "T is a long way from H."

"Oh, I guess I had the wrong drawer."

"Miss Warwick, don't think you're the first to try and find out what the notorious T stands for. We've all tried –

even me. Believe me, nowhere in that overstuffed file is a hint of the famous T. Dr. Barton is the only one in this building who really knows what the T is for. For you and all of us, it's just JT."

"Just like you told me, Jay. So all I said was, 'Thanks, Mr. Johnson.'"

Luigi Bono came on the scene in Jason's junior year. He and his dad arrived from Philly as a result of a job change in a company that made door closers. Luigi was of small, slight build and caused no small stir as a result of the quarter inch bolt in his tongue. He quickly found a mentor in JT and it wasn't long before the two became the fuel of conversations for some, and disgust for others. To Jason it seemed that in Luigi, JT had found a soul mate he could control and train to be his lackey.

Halfway through the second semester, in Mr. Melbourne's Social Studies class, disaster struck when he announced the annual term paper research project. "A term paper is just that. A paper of at least eight, but not more than ten pages. You've all had keyboarding in computer classes, and know your English and composition – use them. A paper needs to come in neat and have a creative title and cover. Look for the correct format in your texts or online. If you want to submit it on a CD, I can work with that. We old folks, like granny, had to do papers on typewriters. Any of you ever seen a typewriter?"

Three hands went up.

"Believe me, you've missed the thrill of your life. You're lucky you have the computer and that delete key. Use computers here in the room, the school library, the library downtown or, of course, your own laptop.

"A serious word of caution here when you're online.

Don't drift into kinky town. As if I have to tell you how to do that. You know – porn and other nasty stuff. Once you start to wander into that village, your computer will tell on you. It will bring up all sorts of bad stuff and ads when you turn it on.

"Folks discover that for themselves, one way or another, especially if you're networked into their computer. Once you get started down that slippery slope it's hard to stop. Think you can erase it? Forget it. It's locked in that computer like every wayward thought you've ever had is locked in your mind. A forensic computer researcher can find anything you ever did on your computer. Make yourself stay on task. Learn it for your school work, career, and all of life."

Sitting in the class, Jason thought, *Boy, there it is again. Learn this stuff for life; this time from Melbourne.*

"Here are the details. Do the paper on any Revolutionary War personality, man or woman, except Washington, Adams, Jefferson, or Franklin."

"Who's left?" Travis asked, with a voice that stopped three feet from him.

"Do your research wherever you can find it. Books, DVDs, internet, or at the County Genealogical Society downtown. Irene Hart and Bertha Phillips, two of my old former teachers, get a kick out of helping kids discover what they can find – and you can't.

"And whatever you do, don't take a short cut and plagiarize. That means copying someone's paper all ready on the internet."

JT turned around and looked at Jason with eyes lit up like a Christmas tree.

Mr. Melbourne continued. "I don't know *every* paper that has ever been done on Revolutionary War people, but if I even sniff plagiarism, you'll have a very bad day."

JT's lights went out.

"Any questions?"

Questions lasted until the bell rang and the demoralized students left the classroom.

Chapter Twenty-One

While walking home, that same day, JT caught up to Jason. "Greene, I gotta talk to you about this no dad thing. Tell me again how do you make it without him? You don't get into trouble like I do all the time. I'm almost always in trouble or on parole"

Jason nodded to the other side of the park and found a low railing around some bushes where they sat down. JT lit up a cigarette.

"It's not easy for me either, Joe. I remember a lot about him. He died when I was thirteen. I remember all the things he did for me and things we planned to do together. We even went on a wilderness canoe trip, just the two us, a year before he died."

"No kidding. What's a canoe trip?"

"Know what a canoe is?

"Don't get smart, Greene. Yeah, I know what a canoe is. Its boat made out of a tree."

"Well sort of. Nowadays they're usually made out of plastic or aluminum."

"Greene, you're insulting me. I do know a few things."

"Sorry. Well, a wilderness trip is a day or many days just canoeing in the wilderness from lake to lake, and living off stuff in your backpacks. There is literally nothing around but lakes, trees, sky, and bugs. Oh yeah, we sit around a fire after dark."

"Sounds like it's not for me."

"Yeah, well the things we did and talked about on the trip are still important to me today. What do you remember about your dad, Joe?"

"You're the only kid in school that knows my first name; don't push for the last. I never saw my dad after I was seven. I barely remember anything about him. I don't want to go there."

"Is he dead?"

"No, he's *not* dead! Don't push it, Greene."

"I remember my dad telling me how life will get tough in the years to come." Jason shrugged. "And now I know what he meant. I think it will even get tougher. He left me with things like, 'suck it up and tough it out.' And words like 'No matter how bad things get, it won't always be like that.' He left me with a lot of hope."

"You don't know how lucky you are. All I got was a 'Shut up' or 'Get outa my way';' usually with the back of his hand or a belt. You got a good mom, and that neighbor, what's his name?"

"Mr. Carlson. Yeah, he's really been a help to me. I wish you had someone like that."

"I do too. But, Greene, I think it's all over for me."

"What do you mean?"

"Maybe this is something only you'll understand."

Wonder what he's going to con me into this time.

"I'm gonna quit."

"Quit what?"

"Quit this stupid school thing. I'm gonna quit school."

Instinctively turning to his friend, Jason grabbed JT's

arm – which he quickly realized was a mistake knowing no one, no one, touched JT, certainly not affectionately. "Joe, you're almost through your junior year. Only one more to go."

"You telling me I can't"

"What brought this on all of a sudden?"

"It ain't all of a sudden. I been thinking about this a long time. This term paper trash about the Revolutionary War just put me over the edge. Without Washington, Adams, and Jefferson, who's left? Who was this Franklin guy anyway? Another president? All I know about Franklin is that once he flew a kite and it's the name of the empty store me and the old lady live above."

Still perched on the railing, Jason went on, "Please don't quit, Joe. I know school is tough for you. I'll help ya."

"You ain't got the time, and school's not all that easy for you either. Besides, your mom wouldn't let me study at your house anyway."

"We can study in the library at school, or at the Junior College – even a back table at the Dawg Hause. Doug likes to have people around the place during late hours."

"Give it up, Greene. Thanks anyway. If anyone would help me it would be you, but your friends wouldn't like it."

"We could work something out."

They started walking again.

"What would you do?" Jason asked.

"I can get a job with my uncle Gary in construction. He works in Florida. At least I can get out of this cornfield."

"Wish you'd think more about it."

"I done all the thinking there is to think. Things just don't work out for me. Did ya know I spent last weekend in jail? They couldn't find the old lady."

"You in jail all weekend? I didn't know that."

"Read your paper, Greene. When Mom found out all she said was, 'You're getting just like your father.'"

"Your dad in jail?" Stopping again, Jason looked closely into JT's shallow gray eyes, and tilting his head slightly in some attempt to show warmth, "Joe, what's the deal with your dad?"

"Careful, Greene, don't go there. How many times do I have to tell ya?"

"You sure are tough on this name thing."

"You would be too, if you knew. Believe me, you don't want to know right now. When we're old, I'll tell ya – maybe."

"There are other people in my life who get involved," Jason said. "Sometimes more than I'd want them to. Mom's always there. Mr. Carlson seems just to know when to come around, and church is starting to make sense. I really feel people care about me."

"Don't get religious on me, Greene."

"Joe, I'm not getting religious. Everybody speaks up with their two cents worth, and I'm just doing the same. Free speech ya know. You always make use of that."

"Well, I never knew anything about my dad and I sure don't know what it's like to have someone care about me – except you maybe. At least you talk to me. The old lady's always working and going around with her friends, and I'm on my own. Once in a while she brings her boyfriends home and they give me the creeps. Sometimes she even locks me out of the apartment. I spent lots of nights sitting on those back wooden steps, sometimes even slept there. I learn things from older guys, and when I found how to work the internet on my used computer, I learned a lot more. Don't try and talk to me any more about quitting school."

"Wow, for a man of few words, you sure laid it all out

just now."

"Yeah, I know, but I gotta talk to someone once in a while, and you're the only ear in town that will listen to me. Tomorrow I'm a free man. I know what I'm doing. I can do anything I want. Who do I see about quitt'n?"

Chapter Twenty-Two

After dinner that night, as Jason and his mom were clearing the table and doing the dishes – another job he knew his mom would never let him out of – Jason lamented the assignment for Social Studies class.

"Mr. Melbourne wants us to do a term paper on a Revolutionary War person other than Washington, Adams, Jefferson, or Franklin. Travis wondered who else is there, and I'm wondering too. JT quit school today because of it."

"JT's in for a tough haul, but we expected it sooner or later didn't we? I'm surprised he made it this far."

"I tried to talk him out of it, but he has his mind made up"

"Son, I know you want to help people, but there are some that just seem not to want any help. Go upstairs, open your laptop and put in Revolutionary War and see what drifts up. There were women back then also."

"Aw, Mom." Jason took his time getting upstairs, putting off the school work as long as he could.

More than once he could hear his mom's voice drifting up the stairs. "Playing games, or the assignment? Got a man or a woman?"

"I'm working on it, Mom."

Working was not the correct verb. With one elbow on the desk and his chin in his hand, pecking at the keys and pushing his finger around on the mouse pad, his thoughts wandered from Sharon Warwick to JT quitting school, back to Sharon Warwick, and everything in between.

Suddenly his spine went straight, eyes bugged out, neck stretched forward, and he lost his breath. A name crossed the screen that looked familiar. Greene. Major General Nathanael Greene.

"Wow!" he said in a loud voice as he stood up and knocked the chair over.

His mom must have heard it down in the kitchen. "What was that all about?"

"I think I got my man, Mom."

"Tell me about it later."

Without answering, he began to read and soon became an obsessed man on a mission. As he read the biography, he came across a bit of information that made him jump up, knocking the chair over backwards for the second time.

"What's going on up there? Since when does homework get so noisy?"

"Tell ya later, Mom. I got research to do."

His mom's answer was faint. "I wonder what inspiration struck you this time. Can't ever tell with you, son."

At ten-thirty PM he heard his mom coming up the stairs and stop outside his room. She must have seen the light shining under the door. She knocked gently.

"Come on in, Mom."

For the next ten minutes, Jason found words of excitement rolling out faster than a kitchen gadget salesman as he told his mom of his find. He kept going until she stopped him with the usual death knell to a high school kid. "Go to bed. Tell me more tomorrow. Now turn the light off."

"Yeah, yeah, but you wouldn't believe this guy."

"Son, don't tell *me* – put it in your paper. Now is the time to go to bed."

"Yesss, Mom."

For the next few days, Jason was a wound-up student that classmates, teachers, his mom, or the Carlsons told him they'd not seen before. He risked life and limb by touching a raw nerve for the first time in asking Alice for a day off from work at the Dawg Hause to visit Irene and Bertha at the County Genealogical Society, downtown.

While searching Nathanael Greene on different websites, the ladies told him they'd found an even bigger surprise than Jason had on his own. They told him that they'd discovered, by following generational lines, Jason Greene of Prairie Heights was a seventh generation direct descendant of Major General Nathanael Greene.

"Boy," Jason said jumping up, "this really touches home, doesn't it!"

It seemed to Jason that Irene and Bertha could hardly contain their own emotions on the discovery. Holding his smooth bold face in her aged-wrinkled hands, Irene said, "Jason, did your dad know this?"

"I don't think so. He never said anything, so I guess he didn't. Don't tell anyone just yet. I want to do that."

After work on Saturday, at another barbecue at the Carlsons, with Sharon Warwick there this time, Jason unloaded his discoveries to the grinning people around him. "Get a load of these statements. I'll only give you a few; the rest you can read in my paper when it's done. General Greene was one of the most valuable generals of the war. He controlled Boston after the British evacuated it. He and Washington were the only generals that served throughout the entire war. He donated his time and fortune to the country. He fought so many battles in the south that Georgia gave him a plantation after the war. Get this: he was so trusted and important to Washington that George made it known if he didn't survive the war, General Greene would take his place. Other generals on Washington's staff were jealous. Coach would like this guy. After losses on the battlefield, he'd say, 'We fight, get beat, rise up, and fight again.'

"After the war he received the Congressional Gold Medal, the highest award, and then went to that plantation in Georgia. He had six kids, but died at forty-four from a stroke. There are more than thirty-three books about him. I wonder how far he would have gone if he lived."

Jason saw his mom and the others looking more than stunned at the enthusiasm of this kid in front of them. "You guys still don't know two bigger bombs yet."

"Well, what else is there to know about this guy?" Sharon asked.

"Hold on to your wicker chairs. Irene Hart and Bertha Phillips down at that society place discovered I am a seventh generation direct descendent of Major General Nathanael Greene through his oldest son, George Washington Greene."

Jaws at the table fell in unison at the news.

"You people look funny, but you haven't heard the best yet."

"Well, how do you top that?" Sharon asked, grinning.

Rising to his full six feet and pointing to his notes, Jason blurted out, "We have the same birthday, July twenty-seven. Get that, Mom? July twenty-seven. How neat is that, huh? That's because of the older calendar they used when he was born. It's good enough to make me famous, right?"

Jason went on to finish the paper that he felt was one of

the turning points in his life. He titled it, "The Greatest Forgotten Hero in American History." From that time on, he became more interested in school and particularly in Social Studies. He appreciated Mr. Melbourne more than just a teacher for his help on the paper. Jason now looked forward to college and some direction in the service of his country.

In January of his junior year, Coach started to get on Jason about looking for a college or university that offered scholarships in football. "There are a lot of them, and I think you could use some help."

"Yeah, Mom and I were talking about that the other day. Where do I start looking? What can you do to help me?"

"I'll be more than glad to write letters of recommendation. And don't forget you already have your name on the short list of some coaches all over the state. So do the others of your football foursome. Too bad all four of you don't want to stay together."

"Coach, that would be nice, but I think we've had our fifteen minutes of fame. Besides, Chris Young has his mind set on a Christian college in Minnesota. Another thing, Coach, I can join the National Guard right after high school, go to boot camp, and get financial help for college through them. It will also get me a start on working up the ladder to be like my dad."

"Spoken like a guy with a plan."

One evening at home, in a moment of great confidence, his mom Michelle said she could sense the years slipping by as he grew in height, strength, and a bold frame like his dad. "Jay, I know college will separate us, and it won't be easy for me. Since your father died I've depended so much on you. Have you noticed?"

"Yes, I have, Mom."

"But I've also tried to prepare you to be independent."

"I figured that out a few months ago when you started to make me wash my own clothes. It used to be cool, working the machines, but in a few days it got boring and a bother. You make me do my own laundry and make me do more things here in the kitchen."

"Get used to it, son. You'll have to do all this in college."

"Yeah in college, but kids don't have to do this at home."

"In this home, this kid does. This one also learns how to iron what needs to be ironed, and go out and buy groceries. You've been making your bed every day since you were four. Don't forget that."

"Hey, that's right. Why was I made to make my bed? Other guys didn't do that when they were four. They *still* don't. I bet JT has never made *his* bed."

"You want to live like JT?"

"Ya got me there, Mom."

"Making your bed was just one of the early training things your dad and I had you do. See, when you make the bed you've accomplished something early in the day. It sets the rest of the day in order. Did you know your dad did his own clothes at times and ironed his dress shirts? Even when I was around?"

"He did? Well, it stays a big secret, huh?"

"Okay, a secret, but this mother's kid will know how to take care of himself."

"Sounds like something Dad would say. You two were really made for each other."

With those words, his mom threw her arms up and around him. "Oh, son, I still miss him so much, and you look like him more all the time. You even have his streak of independence in you that give me these new gray hairs."

Chapter Twenty-Three

After a rare evening baseball game in April, Shawn, Tim, and Jason stopped off at the Dawg Hause for the usual Friday Fry Fest with a lot of their friends. After more than a sack of potatoes, a bunch of grease, ketchup, and salt, little by little the crowd faded away into the night leaving the three sitting by themselves in a booth.

"Hey, the night's still young and tomorrow's Saturday," Tim said. "Let's do something more – something over the edge."

"Like what?" Jason asked.

"Watch a wild movie at someone's house."

Snapping his finger, Shawn said, "I'll bet we could go to JT's place. His mom works night shift at the factory this week and he's asked me over a couple of times. Besides, he's on probation again – I know he'll be home."

Jason hesitated in his agreement, but caved in to Shawn and Tim with the words, "I guess it won't hurt; just once."

The three jumped into Jason's Big-G and drove to JT's apartment above the old, empty and still unsold Ben Franklin store. To get to the apartment from the alley, they had to climb a straight long old rickety weather-beaten wooden stairway. Tim knocked on the door and they heard

JT yell, "Come on in, it's open."

Walking in they noticed a smelly and cluttered kitchen, then in the other room, JT lying on a tattered couch, with Pedro Perez the local tattoo artist plying his trade by carving a lightning bolt in the back of JT's right leg.

"Since when do you make house calls, Pedro?" Shawn asked.

"Ever since JT told me to; and the price is right."

"How much is this costing?" Jason asked.

"Like you should care?" JT fired back. "But if you, the lawyer, must know, eighty-five bucks."

"Wow, eighty-five bucks for something you'll hardly ever see is a lot of money."

"Greene, there you go again, poking your nose into my business. You *will* be a lawyer some day! I think I could use you a lot. You should get a tat, Greene. It'll make you a man. Pedro could give you a nice cross with a halo on it. He could do it for you right now, here, tonight. Roll up your sleeve."

"Very funny," Jason said.

"Hey, why'd you guys come up here anyway?"

"You've always been asking us to come over to see movies. You're not doing anything, so why not now?" Shawn said.

"Yeah, yeah, okay, okay. Make yourselves comfortable. Find a place to sit."

The guys had to step around spilled oil and motorcycle engine parts all over the floor. Jason didn't like the way the place smelled of smoke, or the way the dumpy place looked. From the dead beer cans lying around it was obvious JT and Pedro had been drinking. Better judgment told him now was the time to leave, but peer pressure leaned on him, and won. Jason sat down in a ratty once overstuffed chair. *Wonder if something's going to run out of this thing.*

With a demanding voice, Tim asked, "You got beer here?"

"Sure, we always got beer here. Mom likes it when she gets home from work. If you want some, you gotta pay for it."

"Great," Shawn said, "I'll have some."

"Me too," Tim said. "How 'bout you, Jason?"

"Nah. What kind of movies you got?"

Tim put on a DVD and they all settled in to watch. Shawn and Tim slouched down with their feet on what once was a fine coffee table. With beer cans and bummed cigarettes from JT they looked, felt, belched, and acted like red necks twice their age. Jason felt uncomfortable just by being there and watching the XXX rated movie. *I'm out of it when it comes to this stuff. They seem to be having a good time.*

About halfway through the movie, Pedro finished with the tattoo. "Time for me to go. Eighty-five big ones."

JT got his greasy Levis off a nearby chair and took the cash out of a pocket.

Without thinking again, Jason said, "Where'd you get money like that?"

JT threw him a look with a dagger in it. "Officer Greene, don't ask. You don't want to know. You do have a thick head, don't you?"

Jason realized he had stepped over the trusted line – again.

Soon Shawn and JT started to press on Jason's restraint about not drinking.

"Aren't you gonna have at least one beer?"

"No. You guys know I'm not into that. Why the push?"

"Jay, you're with friends. No one will know what goes on in here," Shawn said.

"Yeah, what goes on in my crib, stays in my crib. I'll even let you have the first one free," JT couldn't help adding.

Trying to shake off his stuffiness, Jason said, "Well maybe just a little. Not a whole can."

One movie turned into three. A little beer turned into four cans. As the evening went on, the movies, cigarettes, and beers all blended into an ambiance of forbidden joy.

"What you gonna tell your mom about the empty beer cans?" Shawn asked.

"She don't care, as long as there are some left over and you keep paying for 'em."

"She really doesn't care? We're minors. We're not twenty-one."

"Just don't do anything stupid on the way home. You guys won't be seeing me again. Tomorrow I'm off to my new job in Florida."

They had a toast to JT and his new job as the clock left Friday in the smoke and turned into Saturday morning. Jason finally spoke through a thin layer of courage. "It's time for me to go. You guys with me, or you gonna stay?"

"I guezz we gotta go. You're driving," Tim slurred.

Jason didn't want to admit it, but he had never had any beers like this, and now found himself about to drive and knowing he shouldn't. Drinking and driving were big issues in Driver Education classes.

When he stepped outside into the cool spring air he felt better, and decided he could handle the driving thing. Tim and Jason made it to the bottom of the steps okay, but Shawn stumbled twice and sunk some slivers deep into his hands when he tried to catch himself on the old railing.

Together, they made it to Shawn's place, then Tim helped navigate to his own house as Jason drove the Big Green through the streets, with them both watching the lights.

The last six blocks to Jason's house was a long, slow, and deliberate drive. Jason had to think hard for every decision and move he made, and it didn't help having guilt chew at his brain. It was hard for him to figure what red lights were stoplights, taillights, or just advertising lights.

Finally turning into his driveway, he thought the houses seemed awfully close together. For a minute he considered parking on the street. *That won't work. I'd just have to explain it to Mom in the morning.* With slow calculated determination he guided Big Green down the center of the driveway. Soon he felt the truck slow down without using the brake as it scraped something on the right side. The scraping continued to the end of the house, but he got the truck into the garage and stopped when it pushed over some boxes in front.

Getting out and looking at the right side of the truck, he saw deep scratches and no mirror. Looking at the house, he saw long green scrapes in the new siding. *Oh, no. How am I going to tell this to Mom?*

He didn't have long to wait or to think up a story. His mom was standing on the back porch leaning on his post.

"Oh, son," he heard from a deeply disappointed voice. "Where have you been?"

"Shawn, Tim, and I were at a friend's houze to see some movies after the game. Guezz it got late."

"Whose house?"

Jason desperately wanted to create a good lie for his mother, but there was no time and too much honesty built into his head. No lie would work here.

"JT's place, Mom."

"Oh, Jason." Reaching up to touch his shoulder and obviously smelling the beer, his mom hugged him with the words, "Get to bed, son. We'll talk about this in the morning."

Tired out, and feeling like a frightened boy with a very hurt mother, he walked into the house, stumbled up to his room, and fell asleep on top of the large fluffy comforter on his bed before he could take his shoes or clothes off.

The aroma of hickory bacon floating up from the kitchen pried Jason awake with a deep sense of remorse for what he had done the night before and how he hurt his mother.

After a quick shower and putting on clean clothes, he slowly walked down the stairs in his white socks, not knowing what was going to happen when he stepped into the kitchen. He thought he'd be accosted by an angry woman, but Swedish pancakes? Hickory bacon?

"I don't get this," he said, standing in the doorway. "Looks like some kind of a reward."

"Not a reward. Just good fuel for an open conversation."

Jason's chest heaved with relief and a special rebirth of appreciation for his mother. *I guess I've given her some gray hair since Dad died.*

As he sat down, he said, "Mom, I don't know what to say. I'm sorry? I've learned my lesson? I know I hurt you? I've betrayed my promise to Dad? Or should I say nothing and just let you rip on me?"

After a minute of silence, "As usual, son, you've climbed into my heart again. I don't know what to say either." She came over and stood behind him and placed her arms around his broad chest, and he could feel her bury her face in his freshly washed very dark hair.

"Son, when I saw you last night, memories of your dad coming home like that came back to me. This morning when I woke I wanted to kick in the door to your room and clear your mind with a few well chosen words. Then I thought, you've been through so much these past few years and were doing so well. Maybe you had to stumble sooner or later. So right now I'm more frightened than mad."

Jason stood up quickly, whirled around and crushed his mother to him tighter than he ever had ever done before. "Mom, I can see what I've done to you, and I want you to know as fast as this problem came on, it's gone. I never want to put you through anything like this again. I will never repeat this act."

"By the way you're shaking, son, I think I'll let the events of last night and this morning rest in that promise."

"You've got my word, Mom."

"That's good enough for me."

"Let's just keep all this between us and the insurance company, can we? I do have some property damage insurance. By the way – how did you know I hit the house? You were on the porch so fast."

"I'm a mom, and when you're not home at such a late hour, I don't sleep very well. When the house shook I thought a truck hit it – I guess one really did."

Jason lowered his head and looked at the hardwood boards on the floor to escape his mother's eye.

Chapter Twenty-Four

After breakfast and a healing time between mother and son, Jason went out to check on Big Green. Stepping off the porch he saw John Carlson running his hand over the green scratches in the siding on the house. *So much for just Mom and me knowing about this.* For a second they just looked at each other.

"Bet there's a story behind this," John said.

"Yeah, but it's my secret." *I should have closed the garage door last night.*

"Not much of a secret, Jay. These marks are trying to say something." Looking into the garage, John continued. "And it looks like Big Green is finishing the story."

"Mr. Carlson, I'd rather not talk about it. This is between Mom, me, and the insurance company."

"You don't want the insurance company in on this. You'll have to fix this one. I'll help you. We can —"

"Please, Mr. Carlson, I can handle this myself." With those cold and harsh words Jason turned and stomped back into the house – abusing that kitchen counter again, this time deliberately in anger.

"Mom, why does Carlson think he can always tell us what to do? Why does he have to play dad to me all the time? Why can't he just mind his own business?"

"Jason Marc Greene!" his mom shot back. "John doesn't want to be your dad. He knows he can't. But you have to admit he's been about the best thing you've had going for you these past years. I'm surprised you're reacting like this. He means a lot to you, and you know it."

"He said the insurance company shouldn't know about this. How are we going to get all this fixed?"

"Maybe he knows how it can be worked out."

"Well, he can just keep out of my affairs from now on!"

Nudging him to a chair, she said, "Son, cool down. Think about all this. John can help you if you let him."

For the first time in either of their memories, Jason resisted her and headed back to the door.

"Not this time. I'm going to the mall and walk this off."

"Good idea, son. Maybe that will help. Be careful, in your state of mind."

Because of the shared driveway, it was difficult to be in the area without seeing each other. John was painting his garage, a job that he and Jason started together a few days ago. Jason walked briskly into his garage and closed the door. Once inside, he wired the right door of Big Green, closed and duct-taped the mirror back on. Without a further word, he opened the large door and drove the wounded pickup to the Dawg Hause.

The restaurant held no friends of his at eleven AM Saturday, so he drove on to the Three Oaks Mall where he walked and wandered among the stores and shops. With stooped shoulders and fists shoved deep into his pockets he tried to sort out last night, this morning, and his unusually harsh words with his neighbor.

He thought back, with the help of a pounding headache,

to the night before at JT's place and the drinking he had done. The thoughts gouged a deep guilt trip on him as he remembered the promise to his dad that he would not drink. He felt the urge to hit, kick, or to destroy something. Only a lifetime of physical control prevented him from striking out.

Now on top of all that, he had separated himself from John Carlson, the man he knew that held him together at the news of his dad's death and through the bumps of life he was going through now as a teenager. Walking past window after window he kept asking himself why Mr. Carlson always seemed to be involved in what he did. At a Christian bookstore he saw a large display of books, one with the title, *Because He Cares.*

Staring at the title, Jason's heart melted as the words, "He Cares" answered his questions. The cover of the book showed a young man behind prison bars, and Jason realized he was now in a prison of his own making. Climbing into his bandaged-up transportation, he couldn't get home fast enough. He had some crow to eat and humble pie for dessert – again

As he drove into the driveway, John Carlson was just cleaning his paintbrush and roller after finishing the painting. Jason walked to the door of the Carlson's garage and just stood there.

"Can I talk to you, Mr. C.?"

Without turning around, John said, "Sure, Jay, anytime. You know that."

"Sorry I was such a jerk this morning. I made a mess of things last night and wasted a good day only thinking about myself."

Looking right at Jason, he said, "Some days are like that, my friend."

"Still friends?"

"Always, Jay. It would take more than a few impetuous words to change that."

"Boy, I don't get it. I was downright rude to you when you wanted to help. Why can't the insurance company fix this?"

With the cleanup finished, John motioned Jason to join him on his back porch, now remodeled into a three-season room with red geraniums and four large hanging Boston ferns drifting in the breeze.

"Sit in that chair, Jay. Have a cup of coffee. At over six feet, I'm sure it won't stunt your growth. You're a beginner in this driving experience. For the insurance company to find out you were drinking and driving within your first year behind the wheel, you'd not only get yourself a bad reputation as a driver, but your premiums would go through the roof. They're probably too high for you now, anyway."

"You got that right. Hey, how did you know I was drinking? Mom tell you?"

"No. I'm sure you told her not to. It's just all too obvious. Home late, I mean early morning, beige siding with green paint scrapings on it, broken mirror, garage door left open. And the way you reacted this morning. Might as well have been on FOX news."

"Oh, Mr. C., was I drunk?"

"I don't think you were stoned out of your mind, crawling on the ground drunk. Buzzed maybe, but you did show poor judgment and did drive into a house. Thank goodness you weren't as drunk as that kid from Ravenswood a few years ago. I think he's still in prison. He killed a woman after just a few drinks."

"Prison? Killed a person? From just a few drinks?" Jason could not believe just a few drinks would get a guy in prison.

John explained, "Drinking is a joke and a fun time for a

lot of people, especially kids your age. Not many realize the end result could be misery for you and your family. I heard that kid from Ravenswood was a nondrinker and it was his first time too."

Leaning back in his chair, shaking his head, and running his hands back and forth on his long thighs, Jason said in a deep sigh, "On the canoe trip before he died, Dad told me about his drinking days and how bad they were. I'm stupid for drinking. I promised Dad I'd never go there. And now look what I've done." He could feel himself breaking down like he thought he'd outgrown, but he continued, "I let Dad down. I betrayed him. I lied to him. If he was here now, I couldn't face him."

"We all stumble and fall from time to time, Jay. We're not perfect. Your dad would be the first to understand your fall, don't you think?"

Jason thought for a moment. "You really think so? You knew him that well?"

"We're just lumps of clay constantly being molded into God's people."

"You think this is God's way of making me a Christian, like Mom and Dad?"

"Could be. Think God's leaning on you?"

Jason noticed Karen Carlson stepping to the door and probably hearing the conversation. But she quickly backed up, left the house, and went over to spend some time with his mom.

"Yeah, I do, Mr. C. God use a drunk kid?"

"Drinking or being drunk is not the point. God uses many ways to get a kid's attention. This was yours."

"Before I completely mess up my life, show me what you showed Dad. How did you clean up his life?"

"Let's get one thing straight first. I didn't clean up your

dad's life – Christ did. I only introduced him to the Lord. He accepted the invitation."

"Introduce me, Mr. C. After last night and this morning I think I'm ready – if God can use a high school kid."

"Many kids younger than you have been used by God. David in the Bible was just a boy when God used him. Billy Graham, the great evangelist, was just a high school kid, maybe a junior like you, when God called him. You're no different."

"Will I be as good as my dad?"

"That's all up to you and what you make of your life."

"Where do we start?"

John reached for his Bible on the table and handed it to Jason. "It's easier than a lot of people think. It starts with realizing that God has a wonderful plan for your life, a plan He had in place before you were even born, and He wants you to experience it."

"I wasn't planned. I'm sure you know how I came to be."

"I do, Jay, but believe Psalm 139 in the Bible. God knew you even before you got your start from Marc and Michelle. Now, let's get back to today. Years ago in Sunday school you learned the basic and first verse. Here it is in John 3:16. 'For God so loved the world that he gave his one and only Son, that whoever believes in him shall not perish but have eternal life.' Your dad believed that and now he's living in his eternal life. But we're not here to talk about your dad. This is for you today."

"Sounds good so far."

"It gets better. The reason God came to earth in the flesh as Jesus, is so you would have life and have it abundantly. That's from John 10:10."

"If it's God's plan for everyone to have a great life, why doesn't everybody have it?"

"Good question, Jay. Because God is holy and man is sinful, there's a large gap or chasm between God and man. Somehow that gap has to be bridged. We've all sinned and come short of God's glory. That's in Romans 3:23."

Jason let John take the Bible back from him, and his neighbor turned to Romans 6:23 and handed it back to him. "Now read this."

"For the wages of sin is death, but the gift of God is eternal life in Christ Jesus our Lord." Jason looked up in surprise. "What sort of death, Mr. C?"

"When the Bible talks about death like this, it means eternal separation from God."

Jason felt himself take an involuntary sharp intake of breath. "I wouldn't want that, Mr. C. So what are the wages?"

"Wages are what we deserve from the work we do. Death is what we deserve from our sins, but God wants to give us the gift of eternal life. Throughout the ages people have tried to bridge this gap in many ways with good works, religion, philosophy, and all kinds of morality; even giving a lot of money to charities. None of these will bridge that gap. Now read Romans 5:8."

Jason read, "But God demonstrates his own love for us in this: While we were still sinners, Christ died for us."

"What do you think that means?"

"It means while I was messing up my life last night, God was still loving me and the other guys too, I guess."

"Right on. Christ bridged that gap. Jesus said in John 14:6, 'I am the way, and the truth and the life. No one comes to the Father except through me.' Jesus is the only way over the separation from a holy God. A lot of people don't like such a narrow point of view, but that's what *Jesus* said, not me. Jesus is the only bridge over that chasm between God and us.

"Now get this. All this is not because of anything *we* did. It's only because of the love and grace of God. It goes back to John 3:16 in that God loves us so much He bridged that gap by sending Jesus to die for us. The only way we get over that gap is to accept His gift. That's it, Jay. Just accept God's gift of grace and life. Are you ready to accept God's gift?"

"It makes so much sense when it's pointed out like that. Yes, I am."

"If you're sincere, pray this prayer after me."

In a natural move, Jason leaned forward and closed his eyes.

John started. "Dear God, I admit I'm a sinner and I need Your forgiveness."

"Lord, I'm a sinner and I need Your forgiveness."

"I am willing to turn from my sins."

"I am willing to turn from my sins."

"I believe You died on the cross for me and rose from the grave to save me."

"I believe You died on the cross and rose from the grave to save me."

"I now invite You, Jesus, into my life and I want You to be my Savior and Lord."

"Now I invite You, Jesus, into my life and I want You to be my Savior and Lord."

Jason felt his inner turmoil relaxing, his heart resting. The failure of last night and the harsh words of this morning left his thinking. He felt an end to many struggles, doubts, and fears he held within himself. He looked at John and saw a peaceful look on John's face and moist eyes.

"Is this what changed Dad's life?"

"Exactly the same thing. In fact, you're sitting in the same chair he sat in."

At those words, even though he was a junior in high school and considered himself an adult, Jason fell into John's arms just like he did on that awful day of the news of his dad's death.

"Thank you, Mr. C. How can I really thank you?"

"Don't thank me, Jay, thank God. He did all the work. Your part is to know how God can work in your life. Know the Bible. Read it daily or as often as you can. It will actually build strength in your faith."

Over the following week and months after his spiritual birthday, Jason made sure he started to read the Bible, starting with the book of John, which was what his neighbor suggested. John gave him a booklet of Bible reading notes, with a portion for each day. As he worked through the planned readings with his father's Bible, Jason began to feel how God really did love and care for him.

Chapter Twenty-Five

Now a Christian in the last half of his junior year, Jason felt he had more to live up to and a deeper responsibility to things he did and thought. But life didn't change all too much. No fireworks or earth shaking events like he had heard in famous people's testimonies or those he read about. His routine was the same; friends were the same but he noticed the language he was used to, and heard around him in school, seemed harsh and useless much of the time. Cussing in the vocabulary of his friends, Travis, Shawn, and Tim, began to bother him, where before he just accepted it as normal.

Jason told his friend Chris Young one day, "When I was twelve I remembered a big change in Dad's life when he became a Christian, but I don't feel anything like that in my life."

Within a few days John Vardeen, Jason's Sunday school teacher, heard from Chris that Jason had surrendered his life to the Lord, but was wondering why things didn't change a lot for him. During Jason's break one day at the restaurant, John Vardeen told him, "The reason you aren't feeling a dramatic change is because you were brought up in a mostly morally clean home. You didn't carry the baggage others do when they receive the Lord. Your dad and mom instilled the Christian principles in you.

"You mean *after* Dad became a Christian, don't you?"

"Right, but he always wanted the best for you. The year after your dad's conversion and before his death he did all he could to get you to understand the change in life he found."

"Yeah, I remember starting to go to church and listening to him try and convince me to follow him in spiritual things. A twelve-year-old skull is a hard thing to crack into isn't it? Wish now I had accepted the Lord on the canoe trip. I think he was hoping for that."

"I know he was, Jay. The point is now, your dad set you up and John Carlson brought you home. If Marc couldn't bring you to the Lord, I'm sure he's glad John did. They were good friends."

"Yeah, but look what opened the way: that stupid night in JT's apartment and the drinking. I 'spose you heard about that too. Wish I had a better introduction to the Lord."

"That doesn't matter. The Lord has dug deeper for others."

John Vardeen warned him there were still pitfalls to be aware of. Going from a nice kid to a Christian kid still called for a change in spirit and witness. "If this is all real to you, and I'm sure it is, you'll want to live a life that reflects it. It still won't be easy. Don't be a fence sitter. Think of it. Sitting on a fence, no matter how you do it, is uncomfortable, even hurts. Others will know you're a Christian by the way you resist many of their ways and what you do. They'll watch you like a hawk and wait for you to stumble and fall back into sin or some other disgrace. You may be the only Christian they'll ever know. You'll set the example of what a Christian is. Being a Christian is a high calling, but you'll have a lot of people praying for you the rest of your life. Your mom, the Carlsons, Chris, folks in the church, me, and many you'll never know."

Near the end of his junior year, Jason and his friends started the process of separation by looking into different colleges and universities. Some of them couldn't wait, and others wanted to hang on to the same crowd for ever – like Sharon Warwick.

Gathered around their upper class "reserved" table in the cafeteria the conversation usually went something like this. "Northwest Christian College just north of St. Paul, Minnesota, is my next home," Chris Young had said many times. Ever since he was a freshman in high school and visited a cousin there, it seemed the matter was settled. "I'd like to major in Political Science or business. They have both there."

Travis and Shawn were set to go west; all the way west. They would laugh, "Iowa! We want to be Hawkeyes. We've got some good football scholarships. Chris, Jay, you guys should come with us and keep the great four together. The coaches said they watched us and would really like to have us all," Travis said.

Jason and Chris just shook their heads no.

Jason wanted to go to the big University of Illinois where his folks met, and he thought he'd walk in his father's footsteps on Green Street. As for Sharon, there was no way her parents could get the money for her to go to one of those schools. She said she would have to settle for the local community college which was okay for her and her desire not to leave Prairie Heights. Sensitive to her feelings, Jason was always ready to chime in with, "Thanks to email, texting, Facebook, and other new techy stuff, we can stay in close touch and I'll be home a lot. After football season, that is."

Tim Blake had no problems. With his dad's fortune he could pick a school anywhere in the country, and he did – one in California. "I've got the chance to leave this cornfield, and get as far away as I can, I'm going to do it."

Applications out, letters of acceptance and scholarships coming back, closed out the junior year and filled in most of the summer.

After the Junior/Senior Prom and the short drive to Sharon's house on the corner of Emerald and 4th, Jason and Sharon sat in John Carlson's Escalade with windows down as the cool evening air drifted through, making conversation easy for the two longtime friends. "I had a good time, Jay," Sharon said. "I hope you did too."

"I did. I like our group of friends, especially you."

They turned and looked at each other, leaned over the gap between the seats, embraced and enjoyed a well timed, deliberate kiss.

"I wish nights like this would never end," Sharon said.

Jason responded with, "Wouldn't it be nice if life could always be like this?"

"It all seems so right. What do you think about the rumors we hear about what other kids are doing tonight? You know, the motel ideas."

"They aren't rumors, Sharon. They are *really* doing what we hear."

"Do you ever think about things like that?"

They stopped talking and faced each other for a long moment.

"You don't want to know, Sharon."

"Jay?"

"You – don't – want – to know."

"I didn't know you thought like that."

"Sharon, I'm a healthy sixteen-year-old guy, I think. But to put it bluntly, I'm still a creature of sin, but not a wild beast. God gave me a brain to sort things out. Regardless what I think, I'm responsible for what I do. It's not easy at times – most of the times."

"Jay, we've never talked about these things."

"Well, I do think about that stuff, but God has given me a good friend in Chris to be accountable to. I like to think we keep each other on balance. It's a very difficult emotion to control, and sometimes I wish I hadn't made such a hard promise to Dad."

"A promise to your *dad*? What do you mean? That must have been years ago."

"It sure was. Someday I might tell you all about it. But I promised him I wouldn't take advantage of a girl and embarrass her or family."

"Boy, am I really out of it. I haven't heard anything like that."

"I 'spose it's strange today, and I might be the last leaf on the tree, but I honestly believe sexual relations belong in marriage."

"You must be the only one."

"You know, I think I am – except Chris."

"Oh yeah, Chris."

"Sharon, I like you a lot and it would be easy to fall, but I not only promised Dad I'd be decent, but I promised God too. Without a doubt this has got to be the most difficult emotion and promise a guy can handle."

Leaning her head on Jason's shoulder, Sharon said, "Jay, I'm glad I'm your girlfriend. I feel safe with you."

They left the car and walked to her front door, talked a

little more, embraced, kissed, and kissed again, then each said, "Good night."

On the ride home, Jason thought about the conversation he and Sharon just had and what it meant. After parking the car in the Carlson's garage, he walked to his back porch and held onto his special post. Looking up into the inky black sky full of blinking stars, he said out loud, "Jesus, will I always be able to keep these promises? Dad was right, it's tough."

Chapter Twenty-Six

With the Junior/Senior Prom over, and the "on the edge conversation," with Sharon, Jason watched his junior year come to a close and a very busy summer open up. No trip to Chicago this year. "It's time for this man to put life into high gear," he told everyone.

Three days after his junior year finished, Jason entered the Illinois National Guard and couldn't wait to start following in his father's footsteps. He and a few others from Fox County traveled to Fort Benning, Georgia, where he began his boot camp in the infantry. Jason knew he could have waited and entered R.O.T.C. at the start of college, but he was chomping at the bit to get started, and the recruiter said this would give him a great heads-up when he entered the Guard after high school.

He wanted to work through the ranks and challenges from the "bottom of the food chain," the way he was used to doing things. For some unheard of reason this was part of the Jason Greene psyche only his mom Michelle, the Carlsons, Chris, and some other close friends knew. Some friends of his said they thought joining the Guard like this was dumb. But it was an attitude that teachers, coaches, and other adults in Prairie Heights constantly told him was the right one. No one actually mentioned the word "fatherless," but he could sometimes read it in their words and looks. "The right attitude for a fatherless young man," was what they couldn't or wouldn't bring themselves to say.

When he first slipped his tall six foot plus frame into the uniform at the supply counter, his mind melted into a mystic kinship with his dad. He recalled memories of helping his dad get ready to go to camp when he was thirteen – the last time he would help his dad with anything. Looking into a mirror, he squared himself and lifted his head. His eyes grew moist although he tried not to show any emotion.

"Hey, kid, you okay?" a voice yelled from somewhere.

Nodding his head, "Yeah, yeah, I'm okay. What's next?"

What followed next were ten weeks of basic training that included marching, yelling, classes, rifle range shooting, more marching, dirt, mud, cleaning up, and still more marching and yelling. Basic training had all the stuff at the bottom of the military establishment that he knew was waiting for him. He accepted it all and thrived on it, unlike some others.

The physical endurance of football and other sports in high school helped him in the training. Grappling with ideas and others in basic training, crawling in the dirt under live fire, and the demands of excellence were elements of his life he loved. Echoes of talks with his dad, and knowing the National Guard vocabulary, helped him adjust to this life. His determination to be a part of this kept him ahead of the other recruits. From his records and attitude, the instructors caught on to his goals. He was appointed a leader in his unit.

His Christian foundations and ideals took a beating at first, but thanks to occasional emails to and from his mentors at home he managed to keep his balance. Meeting

Ray Floyd and Dan Satton, two Christians from the Chicago area, helped him survive the challenges of youthful independence. Together the three formed a special fellowship that oiled their fighting machine against Satan.

Mustering out of basic training, Jason returned to Prairie Heights and working at the Dawg Hause. Even though the hours were long and he was on his feet all the time, he felt comfortable in the familiar surroundings. He knew what was going on around the restaurant, and was in control. He was one of the top servers by this time, and was teaching someone else to eat from the bottom of the food chain.

Fitting him into the schedule clearly galled Alice again this year, because she always thought she was the real boss around there. Jason guessed that if Alice didn't admire him so much and enjoy watching him, she'd find a way to let him go so she could get back into control. It seemed she knew that she had no choice in the matter, as Doug was serious on giving Jason the best of the schedule. So Jason returned the favor by working all he could and helping train the new kids, Doug's way – of course.

There was that dog costume that was a big hit with everyone and did so much for the business. Jason got a kick out of fooling around in it and not having people know who was inside the skin – although the height of the doggie probably gave away the secret. When there were formal events in the Stein Banquet Hall, Jason felt he knew just who to use and what to do; even more than Alice.

One day in late August as Jason was taking an order to the kitchen, he heard a familiar voice from the past. "Hey, Greene, you the boss here yet?"

Without looking behind he knew it was JT. His right hand flew out for a handshake before his body turned around and he welcomed the prodigal with a firm grip that bordered on an embrace – that is if JT would have allowed it.

"Really good to see you back, Joe. I've missed you," Jason said.

"Missed me? Never heard that line before."

JT was wearing a deep tan only a construction worker from Florida could wear. His normally dirty blond hair was almost bleach white, and with a beard and mustache he looked like a young Mark Twain with his head in a tight red wrap.

"I have a break coming in five minutes. I want to hear all about your time in Florida."

"Not much to tell. Me and Uncle Gary didn't hit it off. I can't work with a guy like that. He's some kind of a religious freak, always into that Jesus stuff. A week ago he just told me to hit the bricks and go back to Illinois. He gave me two hundred bucks for bus fare and food. Here I am. End of story."

"Even so, I want to hear about it. Have a seat in a booth over there. Coffee's on the way."

Jason noticed that Alice, watching from across the room, seemed to have her mouth sprung open to object, but some wise spirit must have slammed it shut and she retreated to the kitchen, probably to take her anger out on one of the cooks.

Seven minutes later Jason punched out, bought a coke and joined JT in a back corner booth.

"Come back to finish school or get your G.E.D.?"

"Na, but I got me a good job already. I found my place. Nobody else would understand but you. I got me a job working for the city. Working on a local sanitation collection team– a garbage truck to most people."

"Really? You enjoy that?"

"Sure, heavy lifting keeps me in shape. I can throw things around and break stuff, dress the way I want to, swear as much as I want, and the best thing, it pays good. I get weekends and holidays off with pay. Just the right kind of job for me, don't ya think, Greene?"

"Hey, if you're happy with it I guess it fits. I heard your mom was pretty sick. How's she doing?"

"Sick? Heck, Greene, the old lady died a month ago. I was in Florida and didn't know about it for a coupla weeks."

"I'm sorry, Joe. No one should lose a mom and not know about it."

"Hey, your dad died and look at you now, the town's Cinderella."

"That's a little over the edge, don't you think?"

"You ought to see your life through my eyes – pure gold. Hey, gotta go. I got a chick waiting for me in her car."

"Waiting all this time? Why didn't you bring her in?"

Looking around the room, JT said, "She's not the type I'd introduce to you." He sprang to his feet, wrapped his head in his headband and headed for the door, "Thanks for the coffee, Greene."

As Jason watched his errant friend leave he thought, *Someday, God, I'm going to bring that poor beast to Your table.*

With a few free days they had that summer, Jason and the guys still rode their mountain bikes (Jason thought that this was a strange name for a bike in Illinois) to their childhood haunts like the Captain Swift Bridge over Bureau Creek, or the Red Covered Bridge just north of town. They could all drive now, but riding bikes added camaraderie to the old "gang."

Chris Young who worked at a desk in Seymour Franklin's bank always mentioned he needed the biking because of his weight problem. He said he was glad the other guys went along with him.

On one particular day, Jason and Chris were riding the trail along the old canal south of town, just beyond Log Cabin curve. They got talking about doing something big and different as a wrap-up from school before they split for college.

"Jay, let's do something none of us have done before, something to make a memory."

"Let's bike to Minnesota, Indiana, or Wisconsin. That would be something to remember."

"Look at me, Jay. Take a big long look. Does it look like I could bike to Minnesota? Or even Tiskilwa?"

"Why not hitch hike to California," Jay tried. "Dad always told me crazy stories about when he and a friend did that. They even climbed into some cars on the top level of a car carrier and rode for miles, until one of them had to go to the bathroom."

"Well, that would be far out, but I can hear the folks stomping on that idea. Can't you hear them now? 'Not with all the loonies on the road today.'"

"You're right. Let's drop that scheme before we get burned."

A cross country hike or a bus trip to Florida, or east coast, or even Canada and other ideas popped in and out of their heads like bolts of lightning. When they arrived at a bend in the canal and saw a guy and girl paddling a canoe, they suddenly looked at each other with the answer.

"No! No way are you and Chris going all the way to northern Minnesota alone." At his mom's reaction, Jason winched in pain.

"But, Mom, we're responsible guys, you know that. We could do it."

"Sorry I freaked out, son, but two seventeen-year-olds that far away, with no wildlife experience, is *not* a good idea."

"No experience? Dad and I were…"

"Your dad was an experienced thirty-four-year-old and you were just twelve."

"No negotiation on this?"

"Son, a canoe trip is a great idea, and one in Minnesota would be a great post high school experience. Could you think of some others? And here's the kicker – one of the party should be an adult. Think; for obvious reasons. Run all this by John Carlson. There's experience."

"Mom, that's a good idea. How come you're always so smart?"

"It's a mother's gift."

In his room, Jason sulked with the broken remnants of the great idea – canoeing alone with his best friend in Minnesota. His chiming smart phone grabbed his attention. He could see it was Chris. Without a hello, "Well, how did the bomb go over at your place?"

"It went like this. 'Are you crazy? Just you two? I don't think so.' You too?"

"Yep, shot down like a duck. But a ray of hope. She said there should be more than just the two of us, but one must be an adult. Let's talk this over with Mr. C. He's been on a bunch of canoe trips."

In the next few days, before Jason could corner John Carlson, he began to see the whole picture in his mind. Four more, six more? Na, too crowded, too much to organize. Let's see: Chris, himself, Mr. C., if Chris would agree, but who would be number four? Shawn, Travis, Tim, Corbin, or hey? What about JT?

The idea struck so fast and hard, Jason thought the Lord might have laid it on his heart to consider JT. He quickly ran this thought through a pile of pros and cons. This could be a great witness opportunity for all of them. JT could get away from everyone for a while. He could take the physical toughness. But on the other hand could he live with the life styles of Chris and Mr. C.? Could we put up with his language? Who knows what he'd pull that far away from here. Heck, he'd probably be on probation and couldn't leave the state, or couldn't get off the garbage truck. I don't think JT's the man.

Three days later Chris and Jason had their "appointment" with John Carlson. Before they went next door, Jason asked Chris. "Do you think you could accept Mr. C. to be that adult, if he'd do it?"

"Yeah, I thought of him too. Think he would?"

"He's waiting for us on the porch. Let's lay it on him."

After a time of general talking about canoe trips and getting his attention, Jason, the appointed one, asked John Carlson the daring question. "Mr. C., our folks think we should have an adult on this venture. Um, er..."

"What's on your mind, neighbor. Spit it out."

"Okay. Would you be that adult?"

"What took you guys so long to ask? What date do you have set? Who's number four?"

Chris and Jason slouched back in their chairs and just looked at each other with stupid grins on their faces.

"We don't have number four, yet," Chris said.

Chapter Twenty-Seven

When the doors of P.H.H.S. opened to Jason for his senior year, it was like the Red Sea parting for the Israelites. Things felt so different from when he was that timid, frightened little freshman who had just lost his dad. Now he was on top of that food chain, with Sharon Warwick at his side, along with the rest of his friends. His enormous class ring was on Sharon's small finger with the help of half a roll of tape, and her little jewel on a chain swung around his neck.

The crowning glory of status for him as a senior was his position on the football team as one of the captains. Jason and the other varsity players would see the freshmen players trying to play their version of the game, and would laugh and taunt them. One of the assistant coaches had to remind them, "That's just how you guys looked three years ago. A bunch of plucked chickens, we called you. Your job is to show them the right way to play." Then the stinger. "They come to your games, do you come to theirs? Think what your cheering would do for them. I dare ya to be there Saturday."

The varsity team was riding just where Coach told them they would be if they worked together and followed him. Coach was truly the maker of men. The entire team now realized the unified goal they set for themselves years ago. Things were going great for P.H.H.S. football with lots of state-wide attention. Chris told Jason that scouts from many colleges and universities were often in the stands, always unknown to the players. Maybe it was true.

As the season started, Coach told them, "I'm not just dreaming, but you guys have been the absolute best team I have ever coached. We've had the usual ups and downs, but you've been very trainable. That's something most coaches don't get from a team."

The fearsome foursome was in their last year of fame and well polished by this time, but occasionally their heads got too big for their helmets. One loss early that year was blamed on them for hot doggin' a dramatic sack. The other team picked up on their inflated egos and came on with a vengeance that put them in their place with their only loss of the season.

That year each of the four of them had their sights set on different schools, each for their own reasons. Jason heard that one scout told Coach, after a particular game in early October, "I'd do almost anything, legal or not, to get all four of them at my school."

"Not a chance," Coach said. "We've tried to talk to them into doing just that, till our tongues burned. They play and work well together, but their thoughts for the future are as different as night and day. In a way it will be good for them."

Back in Jason's mind, being a Christian was always a force he dealt with. He enjoyed the personal walk with Christ, even though the daily life around P.H.H.S. served up the usual teenage challenges. Many people around town and in other towns around Prairie Heights looked to P.H.H.S. as a model school of clean and bright young people. Jason and

Chris knew their school was no different than some of the scum schools in the conference. There was drinking and drug use, kinky all night parties, pregnancies, fights, and dropouts by the dozen. Being a Christian in that zoo was a fulltime job. In mid October, an event threw the football team and school for a big loss, and smudged the pure image of P.H.H.S.

During third hour on Monday, the P.A. speaker in Clarence Bedford's English classroom came alive with, "Mr. Bedford, would you please have Jason Greene come to Mr. Ragazzi's office right now?"

Shrugging his shoulders, Mr. Bedford looked at Jason then nodded his head towards the door. Jason got up frowning and left the room. In the stairway he met Chris and Shawn walking toward the offices.

"What's going on?" Shawn asked.

"I have no idea. Do you, Chris?" Jason said.

"Beats me. I always get the willies when called to the office. Ya never know what will blow up."

As they approached Ragazzi's office, they could hear loud and angry voices rattling the glass. When they knocked and entered a very angry and out of character head coach told them in a demanding voice, "Sit down, all of you."

The Santa Claus image they saw as freshmen that first day was gone, far gone, but the face was just as red as Santa's would ever be. "One of your famous four is sinking in deep weeds, and I want to know what you three know about this."

Six senior eyebrows rose up; eyeballs bugged out and flashed at each other in pure horror. With a shaking hand, and a face with bright red blood vessels looking like a roadmap, Coach waved a letter in front of them. "You guys know the policy about drinking, drugs, and all that other stuff, right?"

All nodding their heads Yes, answered together, "Sure we do, Coach."

"Well one of your friends just cut you off at the knees."

In total fright and shock, Jason suddenly realized Travis Valdez was missing from this inquisition. "Something about Travis, Coach?" he asked.

"Bingo!" Waving a wrinkled piece of paper in the air, the coach continued. "It sure is. This letter tells me he was seen at Tommy's Tap down in Capital City last Friday night – I mean Saturday morning, about one o'clock. He was drunk as a skunk and doing drugs with a seedy looking crowd including 'Ladies of the evening,' if you three know what they are."

They nodded in silence, afraid to interfere with the rolling rampage. The coach continued in his angry, high pitched and hurt voice. "I don't have the time or reputation for this. Remember what I told you all just a few days ago about being a great team?"

Three heads nodded again like doggie figures in the back window of a car.

"If any of you know the slightest thing about this, speak up, or you'll fall like Valdez – down and out!"

"Now, Coach," the Athletic Director, Angelo Ragazzi, said, "we should check this out some more. Maybe there is a mistake here. The letter is from an anonymous source."

"I *have* checked it out, and there's no more anonymous source. I haven't been head coach around here for twenty-three years without having friends in every closet of this town. I found out who wrote it and was told this was not the first time that boy was in this crowd. He was there alright, and I've had a very bad weekend. Have you boys noticed your friend Travis Valdez is not in school today? His uniform is already in a pile on the locker room floor – right where I threw it. I told the janitor to leave it alone and I'll take care of it when I get good and ready. I want all the teams to see it there, and smell it rot, as a shrine to the fact that I mean what I say."

"Was that necessary?" Mr. Ragazzi asked. "Maybe we should have talked it over with the boy and the school board."

"What's to talk over, Angelo? You're new here this year. You ask these three what the policy is and how I feel about this stuff."

"He's right, Mr. Ragazzi," Chris said. "We all knew it on day one when we were freshmen. We all agreed to it. Coach did the right thing. He had to. Travis knew the rules as well as we all did."

Looking at the coach like a son looking at a hurting father, Jason said in a shaking voice, "Coach, we sure didn't know anything about this, and we're sorry. I know this could wreck the team, but I can speak for all of them when I say we'll work harder for you and the school. You're the one who taught us a team is more than just one guy."

Coach turned away from the boys, walked in a small circle rubbing his chin, then faced Jason and reached up to his shoulders. The seasoned, short and beaten coach said, "What's with you, Greene? What did your dad leave with you? For being the tough and aggressive player you are, you've just been a great comfort to this old angry man. Thank you, son."

Mr. Ragazzi just swiveled in his leather chair and shook his head. "I don't know what I'm going to tell the board. They won't like this."

The Athletic Director didn't have to wait long. In just a few days this all festered again when Travis' father brought him to the school and locked horns with Mr. Ragazzi, Dr. Barton, and Coach. "Let the boy play. One little night out didn't make him a criminal."

"I won't do it again. I can still play the game. It didn't affect my ability at football," a timid voice from Travis said.

"Travis, affecting your abilities isn't the point," Coach told him. "You know the rules like all the others. No drinking and no drugs. If I let you off on this, I'll soon be pulling half the team out of bars all over Fox County. On the first day of training years ago these rules were set down and all agreed to them. When you arrived on the scene you got the word as well, and you signed off on them too. They've worked for all my twenty-three years as head coach. I don't need you to change all that."

"You just throwing him away, Coach?" Mr. Valdez said.

The Athletic Director and Superintendent looked at Coach, waiting for the answer.

"Dr. Barton," Coach began, "you well know I've had to do this in the past, and will probably have to do it in the future."

Ragazzi spoke up. "I think all of us in this room know rules are made to be broken."

He might as well have kicked a bear cub with mama bear nearby. Now bellowing, Coach reached a new octave. "Made to be broken? That's the dumbest thing I've ever heard come from an Athletic Director in my whole life. Rules make the game of football. We pay good money for officials to be right among the players on the field to make them obey the rules. We live all of life under rules."

Keeping the pressure on, Mr. Valdez said, "He'll probably hate football and all sports now, and even drop out of school. Coach, you've just ruined a kid's life."

With a voice now back within its borders, "I'm not the

one ruining his life; that bar and people in Capital City are doing that. My intent and promise to this community is to teach him and all the players through hard lessons that rules make up sports and all aspects of life. Sometimes the harder the lesson, the more wisdom is learned."

"It looks useless to try and talk anymore. This would not work like this in California," Mr. Valdes mumbled.

Under his breath, Coach sarcastically breathed, "California!" Later that day, when Jason heard about this argument he thought, *I figured something like this would blow up.*

In a final desperate attempt to rescue himself, Travis said, "Coach, ask the rest of the team if they want me back, Hey, ask Jason, Chris, and Shawn."

"I've talked to those three, even let 'em in on the details, and they've all backed me up."

Travis and his dad slumped back into their chairs in defeat.

Chapter Twenty-Eight

The next game was a tough one, but the team welded themselves together for the coach and won it 19 to 14. The season was coming to an end, and Jason still thought about how his quiet and contented life differed from the aggression he produced on the field where he had no problems with smashing another player into the ground or separating a quarterback from the ball.

With Travis out of the fabulous four, the other three took it upon themselves to be the force behind their promise to the coach. The season ended at 8 and 1 which took P.H.H.S. to the playoffs and into the championship game on a cold November night in the Capital City stadium.

The game was between the two steaming rivals of Prairie Heights and Ravenswood. The Big Bureau River running between the two towns also separated the two counties and conferences. The bleachers and hard benches in the end zones were loaded with hopeful fans.

Announcers from three different radio stations were excited and using eloquent remarks trying to keep their listeners' ears filled with the pictures throughout the evening. At ten PM the little red lights on the scoreboard pierced the cold and damp dusty air with a score of 7 to 7.

Jason knew the blue collar, working class Ravenswood population always saw the Prairie Heights crowd as the professional smug mugs of the area. In a close game like this, the young players of both teams would do anything just to be able to knock the other out of bragging rights to the championship. But with Ravenswood on the three yard line, and with only four seconds on the clock, oxygen was scarce on the P.H.H.S. Bulldog bench.

As the teams got into their places for the last play, it was obvious to Jason that Ravenswood was getting set up for a sure and easy field goal to put this game on ice and grab a championship from Prairie Heights. With the ball resting on that three yard line in a fourth down situation, the kicker was counting his paces back to the fourteen.

Visions of trophies, parades, and parties were probably dancing in Ravenswood heads. Prairie Heights skulls would be thinking of what it would take to mess up just one more play and put this game into overtime. The Prairie Heights defense didn't have a quarterback to get to this time.

Ravenswood cheerleaders were beyond excited and some fans from both sides began to leave the stands to get a few minutes jump on the traffic as the outcome of the game was as good as settled. The loyal and faithful from both sides took a deep breath as the referees stepped back to their positions. Twenty-two young hearts pounded in both directions as Ravenswood 55 placed his hands on the ball.

The center rolled the ball to fit his grip then lifted it to send it seven yards back to the holder. In the snap, his hands slipped on the damp ball and he swore with one word, informing all players in the tight neighborhood, something's wrong. The low wobbling ball barely made it to the holder who had to reach for it and twist it to the right position, costing a precious second. The confused kicker himself lost a second or two in adjusting his steps to the ball.

At the sight of the ball being snapped, Jason and Chris pushed through the line with their usual thrust, not realizing they had about three seconds head start on the kicker thanks to the bad snap. The kicker finally sunk his right foot into the ball and sent it to the uprights. But not high enough to escape Jason's eight foot five stretched-out jumping reach from deflecting it into Chris' chest. In the melee and confusion that screamed, "Where's the ball?" to players and fans alike, Jason knew that only he and Chris had the answer, but even they were as befuddled as the rest.

As defensive players, Jason knew he and Chris were immediately in possession of an opportunity neither was prepared for. *"Expect the unexpected, then the unexpected will be expected."* Words of Coach on their very first day of football practice as freshmen, years ago, raced through Jason's mind. While spinning around, the boys heard the air horn blast the end of the game, but Jason also knew as long as the ball was in play and not on the ground, the game was still on.

Chris obviously knew the same as he handed the ball backwards and pressed it into Jason's numbers with the words, "I'll never be able to run the field."

Wanting to say thanks, but not having the time, Jason took off for the long run with Chris right behind to block a pursuer – if they ever figured out what was going on.

Adding another second or two to the fray gave the two Prairie Heights Bulldogs a slim advantage for their flight. With a set of goal posts ninety-four yards away in the dark, with nothing in front of him except torn up sod and noise, Jason buried the ball in his arms and started the sprint of his life. The scariest, but brightest moment of his life dawned on him with a flash inside his stuffy and sweaty helmet. *"Jesus, please run with me."*

Jason and Chris were about five yards on their way before other players and fans woke up to the facts and the radio announcers finally figured out how to untie their tongues.

Four Ravenswood Ravens caught on, and were on their way after the two Bulldogs. But a few Prairie Heights players jumped up and wiped two of them out of the race. Jason and Chris got to the thirty-five yard line rather comfortably, but comfort was about to be lost as two Ravenswood runners were closing in on them. Adrenalin with extra effort and cleats digging deeper into the grass the fifty and forty yard line slipped beneath them. Four runners with hearts pounding and pumping blood harder than ever before kept up the race, clawing for one more white line after another

The three radio announcers knew they had to keep talking, but it was obvious through their tumbling words they would rather just watch these four young bucks run this race.

Although the fans of both sides were arguing in unheard of volume, it was silent inside the four helmets. Each of the four runners felt the pressure of the entire season, and most of all, their whole high school reputation in their legs, lungs, shoulders, feet, and stinging eyes. At the twenty yard line Jason not only felt the growing vibrations of impending doom, but also heard the challenging breathing of his enemies. End of the season, end of high school football, and end of the game fatigue reached its ugly arms around his legs, but even in his fear of losing it all, he figured fatigue was clawing at his adversaries' legs also.

Not knowing what white line it was they just crossed, Chris saw he could take one of the runners out so he threw his body in front of the two pounding hoofs, making him crumble in a heap and out of the race. One pursuer jumped over Chris' reach and escaped the tackle and gained on Jason at the ten yard line. Jason felt his jersey being pulled with enough force to bring him down. For a fast second, he thought, *I could quit this race and let him take me down, the game would stay tied and we would go into overtime. I'd still be the hero.*

In a flash of thoughts while twisting his body within two or three steps, he recalled words of his dad from the canoe trip five years ago. *Suck it up and tough it out. No choice, no option, no other way.* He knew if he went down now he couldn't slide far enough to make the goal line. In one of the greatest moves in all of footballism, with Jason's adrenalin running at its peak, and strength coming from sheer determination, he grabbed the Ravenswood player around his waist and carried him, and the ball, three more steps across the goal line and collapsed.

As the two challenging warriors laid there, gasping for breath on the damp ground, the Ravenswood player said between gulping breaths of air, "Great run – Greene."

Fighting to fill deflated lungs, Jason asked, "How did you" – (gulp) "know my name?"

"That's all" – (Huff, huff) "I've been looking at for the last ninety-three yards."

Chris was on Jason in an instant and the two of them just laid there until the rest of the team piled on. Other team players picked them up, yelling, cheering, high fives, and banging chests and helmets together. The Bulldog hero was carried back to the benches amid the noise of a very happy Prairie Heights crowd. Jason saw coaches running to the team with smiles on their faces, rarely seen before this event. Off to the side he saw an older referee bent over and desperately trying to catch his breath.

With a heart pounding with joy, it now broke in grief and tears with the thought, *"Dad, Dad, did you see that?"* Tears flowed freely from his eyes and down his face mixed with massive sweat. No one noticed.

Jason's fifteen minutes of fame turned into a few weeks, with articles in local and statewide papers and letters of congratulations. Jason even had a ten second blurb on FOX NEWS. Clips of the high school phenomena were flashed all over the United States and even some other countries. From many colleges, letters of applications came to the high school and the house. Jason, Michelle, and the Carlsons read them all and tried to decide which ones to take seriously. Inside Jason's heart, he still wanted to go to the university his dad and mom went to, and where they met. The University of Illinois.

When the euphoria of Jason's historic and heroic event quieted down in the few weeks after the football season, Jason clung to some selfish remnant of a swelled ego. Sharon and Chris were brave enough to venture onto that thin, cracking ice and tell him he had to let it go and move on. But at times he felt he could do no wrong, and an idea he had for some time floated to the surface.

Some of the other football players, except Chris, quickly got tattoos to seal their claim to state-wide fame in their hide. When pressured to join them, Jason boldly stated he had another way of making that statement and remembering the prize.

One noon with several football players at their table, Jason said, "I've already started to show my claim to fame. Look at this." He pointed to the patch of skin above his nose where his eyebrows had until recently met. "See this? I'm just going to let it grow so it joins the eyebrows to make one long, strong, and bold statement. You guys get your tattoos; this will be my badge of courage.

"That's sick, Greene," Shawn said. I've never seen that before."

Other players sat back with chins down, frowns on their faces, shaking their heads.

"That's the point – never been done before. Anybody can carve a date in their leg."

"I think it really looks stupid, Jay," Shawn said, shaking his head in disgust. "Who's ever thought of that?"

"Well, I just came up with it," Jason said, with a little brag in his voice.

Jason's best friend, Chris, even said it was stupid. "What does Sharon think of it?

"Ya know, she hasn't even mentioned it. I'm waiting for the day she does. Don't tell anyone, Chris; or you other guys either."

"Okay, okay, but let me know when the bomb goes off. I still think it's dumb," Chris said, again.

It took about a month before his mom noticed it and her first remark was something about finding a razor.

"It's my statement, Mom. All the kids have some tattoo or orange hair, a hat, jacket, or something they think is different. This really is different, don't you think?"

"It sure is. I can't say I like it very much. I think you should…"

"Mom, I'll make you a deal. Let me keep this awhile, and if everybody, everybody, thinks it's repulsive I can easily take it off. It's not like a tattoo or a bolt through the nose."

His mom nodded reluctantly. "You've got a point there. Okay, son, it's a deal. Mind if I don't look at it much?"

"That bad, huh Mom? Almost everybody at school thinks it's dumb or stupid. Even my friends Shawn and Chris. What really makes it so bad?"

"All your friends telling you they don't like it? Doesn't that tell you something? It's not natural. I've never seen such a thing before. It makes you look like..."

"Not natural? Why does the barber always trim it or people pluck the hairs out? I know it makes me look different, but that's the point. It's not as bad as..."

"Stop, my dear impetuous, independent son. I've heard that line before. I don't know why you're going over the edge on this. It's so unlike you, but you'll have to learn the hard way when people laugh at you. You've only got one point in your favor – it's not permanent."

Michelle closed the argument with, "Your mother has spoken. It comes off for your wedding."

"Okay, Mom, off for my wedding." Whatever, whenever, wherever, and with whoever that will be.

One day Shawn couldn't contain himself any longer. At the lunch table he blurted out, "Sharon, you see something stupid on Jason?"

"I don't. What's wrong with him?"

"His eyebrows, girl. Look what he's done."

"Yeah, I've known that for weeks. I think it's cute." She reached over and touched the small clump of hairs.

Jason grinned with that touch. Chris again made his statement about how stupid it was.

Jason finally snapped from all the negative comments. "Boy, I don't get it. Kids get tattoos, earrings, let their hair grow long, get a Mohawk, or even shave their head completely. They wear beards, mustaches, goatees or any hair type in between. Guys wear pants low showing butt cracks and girls wear low cut blouses showing cleavage. They pierce ears, bellies, eyebrows or wear a quarter inch bolt in their tongue. I let a small patch of hair grow between my eyebrows and I've created a crisis in the White House War Room."

"With a defense like that," Sharon said, "you've got to be a lawyer."

During Christmas vacation, after the multi level argument of the eyebrow incident had died down and were mostly forgotten, Jason and Chris got serious about who the fourth man on the canoe trip would be. After tossing around names like Travis – now that the brush with death and the coach had subsided – Shawn, JT, and some others, they decided on Tim Blake. After all, Tim had helped Jason and Chris resurrect "Big Green" from Doug's old pickup a year ago, which showed dedication and persistence. Raising his part of the money for the canoe trip would not be a problem for someone in Prairie Heights with the name Blake.

When Chris and Jason asked Tim to go on the canoe trip, he responded with, "A week long camping trip? I'm for that."

"It's more than just a camping trip. There's a lot of paddling every day and portages between lakes that..."

"Portage? What's a portage?" Tim asked.

"Oh, boy," Chris said, when he and Jason raised their eyes and rolled them back in their heads.

"Well, what's a portage?" Tim persisted.

"That's what you do when you carry all the gear and canoe from one lake to another. You sure you want to do this?"

"Carry all the stuff?"

"Everything," Jason said. "Sometimes several times a day. A canoe trip is not for the faint at heart. There's no chance to turn back. It's kinda like a polar expedition."

"Hey, Tim, if you're really into this, we'll borrow a canoe

in the spring and try all this out on the canal," Chris said.

"I'm into it. I can do it. I can do it. If you guys can do all that, I can too. But do we have to do that canoe thing in the canal?"

"We really have to do that!" Jason said.

Chapter Twenty-Nine

When school started for Jason's last semester, it started with a bang in Mr. Clarence Bedford's English class. While Bedford was scribbling instructions on the white board, Luigi Bono started to bad mouth Colin Tibbles, a new student who came to the school just last year about the same time as Luigi, in a voice only heard by Jason and the other local students near him.

A gentle, large African American kid, smart, well liked, and the last one to be found near a fight, Colin tried to ignore the trash talk concerning his mother. Jason and the other students became increasingly uneasy with the torment being unleashed on their friend, and were holding their breaths watching Colin's dark face go red and hands turn white, reaching the breaking point.

Without warning, Colin got a quick fist into Luigi's ribs, noticed only by those close behind him. That quick jab was an open invitation for the hot blooded Mediterranean, and reason for Luigi to answer with a massive assault. Luigi's right arm crossed over his chest in preparation for a full swinging attack across the aisle into Colin's face. Just as the catapult was released, Jason grabbed Colin's shirt collar and pulled him out of Luigi's reach. The momentum of Luigi's swinging arm, not landing on anybody, carried him out of his desk and onto the floor, hitting his face on Colin's desk on the way down.

Now fully aware of a problem in his flock, Mr. Bedford whirled around only to see a bloody Italian face rising from the floor. As the other students looked on in fake surprise, the disgusted teacher said, "I don't want to hear your story, Mr. Bono. Take a hike to the Dean's office and tell him your story." Pointing to the door, "Leave!"

With only a little snickering, the class was silent throughout the episode. Almost without missing a beat, Mr. Bedford said, "Now, where was I? Oh yeah, in your writing, always keep polishing the 'Pugs,' – punctuation, usage, grammar, and spelling."

In late February a date was set for the four canoeists to make plans for the expedition. A few days before the briefing session, John Carlson stopped Jason in the driveway. "Have you thought out the choice of Tim Blake as the fourth person? He comes from a wealthy, privileged background used to having things being done for him. Are you sure he can put up with the ruggedness of a trip like this?"

"Chris and I have talked to him about that stuff, and he's sure he can handle it. It will be good for him, don't you think?"

"It sure will, but you'll have to step in if he breaks down. Can you handle that?"

"Good point, Mr. C. I think I can."

Three days later, Jason sat with Mr. Carlson, Chris, and Tim at his dining room table and spread out all the brochures, maps, and pictures they received from the outfitters in Minnesota.

"Look at all this stuff just for a canoe trip," Tim said. "Are these pictures for real? Come on, it says, 'So quiet you can hear your own heart beat. Islands and water like a mirror.' Is it honestly like that?"

"Honestly – just wait and see. When it's all over you won't stop talking about it, like me," Jason said.

"For five years," Chris added, "I've listened to all these stories and I've come to believe it. Jay and I have been on the canal a lot of times with Mr. C's canoe, and he knows what he's talking about. I can't wait to get to the real thing."

"The first decision we have to make," John Carlson said, "is how much do we want to get from the outfitters and how much do we want to bring up there ourselves. There are several packages. Just look at these prices."

"Wow!"

"Oh, man."

"You gotta be kidding."

"Add to this the gas to get up there and back, as well as other expenses like food."

They decided on bringing as much as they could and just getting the food for the trip and canoes from the outfitters. As for clothes, Tim claimed all he needed was a couple of shorts and tee shirts.

Jason looked at John Carlson, and laughed. "I guess he doesn't know what the state bird of Minnesota is, does he?"

"What's the big deal about a state bird?" Tim asked.

"It's the mosquito – and they like your blood type. You'll want a couple pair of jeans, a jacket and a sweatshirt."

"Aren't we going in the summer? Why the jacket and sweatshirt?"

"Now I know what my dad had to put up with," Jason said. "Chris, Tim, it might be summer on the calendar, but this is far northern Minnesota. They don't have summer calendars up there. When we're going to rough it like this, we rough it. Sometimes it's cold and other times it can even get hot. Trust me."

With prepackaged food needed, canoes to rent, and gas to pay for, they put the numbers to the calculator. They divided the horrible number by four and ended up with about four hundred dollars each. John Carlson sat back and waited for the decision to change all this and just settle for a week canoeing on the canal south of town. The guys griped and moaned, huddled up like a football team, then said in one voice. "We'll do it. Somehow we'll do it."

It was also decided at the meeting that they would keep moving throughout the week and not stay at one campsite. Tim was the one to blurt out, "I don't want to get bored sitting on a log in one place all week."

John Carlson looked at Jason and raised his eyebrows with a smile on his face. He then brightened the day with the news they'd all share the driving – in his Escalade. Chris and Jason left their chairs over the news. Tim, used to new cars, just shrugged his shoulders. They went through a series of coin tosses to see who would drive first, who would sit where, what CDs to play, and all that other important stuff.

National Guard drills filled one weekend a month for the remainder of Jason's senior year. This busy life thrilled him, but gave Alice no rest in the scheduling at the restaurant. Once she even confided in him that although she liked watching him work, she'd be relieved to see him go!

Throughout the waning months of his senior year, Jason began to feel he had some kind of responsibility to the friends he grew up with in Prairie Heights. Kids he knew in Happy Hands pre-school, elementary, Junior High, and now high school. Some like Sharon, Chris, Shawn, Tim and others became close friends, while others drifted away in disappointed lifestyles. Some moved and others dropped out of school to start parenthood many years before their time.

As a Christian, Jason wanted to share his testimony and witness for Christ, but he just couldn't bring himself to express his message in words. In another encounter with his Sunday school teacher John Vardeen, at coffee time after church one Sunday, John told him, "A witness for Christ doesn't always have to be in words. You can witness loud and clear by the respect you give others, attention you pay to them, or your general consideration and caring. Remember this, Jay, you've cared for JT more than any other kid in school, or even any pastor in this town. God is working in JT's life through you. It wouldn't surprise me if someday you'll lead that kid to the Lord."

Wow, heard that somewhere before.

"Even being clean, deodorized, dressed well, polite, and doing the best you can in your work say a lot. A silent witness speaks loud and clear and is well respected. A good strong Christian witness stands out with a well ordered and disciplined life. Just think of all the respect and tribute your dad received at the funeral. He meant a great deal to a lot of people because, when he became a Christian, he made a difference in their lives.

"All too often today a Christian melts into the unbelieving crowd around them. Too much association and conforming to the world makes the Christian fade away from Christ's call to 'Come out from them and be separate.' Read all of Second Corinthians 6. Romans 12:1 and 2 are good verses for a guy like you to know.

"A good example you've already accomplished is your success in football. You've never been called for unsportsmanship conduct, even though you've really been pounded hard and had some good plays broken up. Another good example of how you're doing is how you're treated over there at the restaurant by customers and other employees. That kind of goodwill doesn't come to slouches. You probably don't know this, but you've witnessed well by the way you've recovered from your dad's death without becoming bitter or blaming God for your misfortune. Some people, kids especially, never get over something like that, and they spend the rest of their lives blaming all their problems on God."

Looking to see if others could hear, Jason whispered to his Sunday school teacher, "In my prayers for about a year after Dad died, I said some bad things to God when I was alone. You didn't see me alone in my room that year after Dad died. I wasn't so good to God."

"We all have times like that, Jay. Another thing, you've made many people all over town proud of you; your mom, the Carlsons, Doug and Alice, me, and many, many more. See, you're doing it right. Just keep it up."

"Thanks, Mr. Vardeen. I'll need that encouragement as I start climbing a new ladder at the university next year."

"Brace yourself, friend. That ladder could be the toughest one you'll climb in your life. Keep in touch."

Chapter Thirty

In early spring, Tim, Chris, and Jason borrowed John's canoe and had their date with the canal to try out their wimpy explorer skills: a few hours canoeing, a night on the old mule path, swimming in the cold water and returning back the next day. All went well except for the lack of sleep because of the animal noises and a stupid raccoon that didn't have the good sense to stay away.

They decided they were ready.

With the end of the school year and his time in high school coming to a close, Jason often reflected on the past four years. When he started school he was depressed and as scared as Ananias in the New Testament, when he was told to go and meet Saul. However, he realized that his father's reputation as a teacher and well liked figure around Prairie Heights did a lot to pave the way for him. Jason, reluctantly at first, eventually stepped into his dad's wake, and the time in high school ended with him in full control of his emotions and willing to take his place in the challenging world.

He never attained top twenty status in his class, but thanks to football, a pleasing personality, and clean moral behavior, he established a rare quality of respect and admiration from faculty and students alike.

During the final three months of school, Jason began to let go of the details in his classes. Senioritis, they called it, and with the end in sight, scholarships in place, the University of Illinois waiting for him, and dreams of the canoe trip taking shape, Jason had a bad case of it.

Mr. Malcolm Williams, the math teacher, literally pulled him aside one day by his arm and said, "Mr. Greene, I don't usually talk to a student like this, but I think you can take it and learn from it."

"What's that, Mr. Williams?"

"I see you sluffing off in these final months, and if you don't get your head back into your school work, you could still lose some of the promised future waiting for you."

"I'm doing that?"

"Yes, and I'm not the only teacher to notice it. You're the talk of the teachers' lounge"

"I hear you. Thanks, I'll work on it."

Jason reflected on this, and could see that this was not interference so much as another adult interested in caring for him, and he determined to get his head back to the work at hand. He put in extra time in studying for the finals and kept himself on track. He knew he wasn't the brightest bulb in the lamp, but he maintained his status with his grade point average.

End of the year activities for the seniors filled Jason's life with fun and hope, but they put a severe hurt on whatever savings he had. The class trip to Great America north of Chicago was just that – great. Jason, Sharon, Chris, and Tim, and their girlfriends, could not go fast enough, or twisted, or up-side-down enough on the rides. Sharon and the other girls tried the best they could to enjoy the roller coaster mania, but after the third beating had to admit they were not built for the abuse. Sharon and the girls enjoyed other rides and the shops.

On the ride home going past Chicago, Jason couldn't hold back. "That tallest building is the Sears Tower, now Willis Tower, the one with the Xs up and down the side is the Hancock. We can't see the el from here or see the lake, but the..."

"Greene, cut with the tour guide bit – no tip in it for ya," came from a disgusted voice tucked far back in the yellow bus. "We've all been to Chicago. No big deal."

Deflated, Jason quieted down quickly and Sharon squeezed his hand in an affectionate show of understanding.

Playing the role of prom-goer again came next, and right from the historic playbook with tux, flowers, pictures, and dancing. It was the evening Sharon said she'd been looking forward to from her freshman year. Jason, on the other hand, thought it was okay. The highlight of the evening, other than Sharon's dazzling appearance, was the use of John Carlson's Escalade again, instead of his mother's Buick. Jason could hardly get his head through the door, but he tried to act humble – unsuccessfully.

After the dance, Doug Hauseman let the kids enjoy several hours of entertainment and more dancing in the Stein Banquet Hall. He paid for a noted band from the St. Louis area and kept the buffet well stocked with things the kids liked, such as their assortment of French fries. It was Doug's big night too.

On this particular night all activities came to a standstill when the high school superintendent, Dr. Cecil Barton, some of the school board members, Alice, and dozens of other adults entered the room to Doug's surprise. A few students, Jason among them, "Dum, dum, de dumbed"

Pomp and Circumstances as they all held a mock graduation ceremony for Doug. Dr. Barton presented Doug with a fully official Prairie Heights High School Diploma. "Based on his outstanding concern for the students of Prairie Heights and years of practical educational experience."

Doug was so overcome he was just lost for any words to say other than, "Thanks." The hall full of City officials, parents, school board members, and students erupted in a deafening roar of appreciation.

At one AM the students filed into four modern charter buses from Peoria and were driven to the Mississippi River for an all-night cruise on the Lady Belle, with food, dancing, and memories to be made. Kind of old fashioned, some thought, but safe and fun none-the-less. Some classmates dodged the buses and disappeared into the night to places unknown and memories not to be spoken of.

Only graduation was left now, which took place on the football field in seventy degree temperature, a gentle breeze, and a fabulous sunset. The speaker told them, "Just like the sun is setting tonight in the west, the sun is setting on this part of your lives. Tomorrow that same sun will rise on a new morning with new promises and you will have the opportunity to make it a dawning of sunshine or storms."

Some students could only think about the end of ringing bells, structured hours, assignments, teachers, and on and on. Others caught the symbol of the setting sun and the dawning of promising tomorrows of their lives with plans for jobs or higher education.

Even though it had been five full years since his father's death, Jason sat in his chair on the field and watched his mother and the Carlsons in the stands. His heart still ached for the one missing from that small group; not even an open seat where he would have been.

Like a great curtain falling with the setting sun, names were read and the procession began. "Timothy Owen Blake – Luigi Federico Bono – Jason Marc Green – Shawn David McClintock – Colin George Tibbles – Travis Juan Valdez – Sharon Beverly Warwick – Christopher Walter Young …"

While sitting on the field one last time, Jason thought of how football and this sod had come to mean so much to him, and how it all helped him rebuild his life. He could see that the hard lessons and strength learned right here on the field bolstered him up and taught him the truth of every word Coach said on that first day.

Jason watched Travis gouge a hole in the grass as a lasting reminder of his presence on the team.

Chapter Thirty-One

At six the following morning, the driveway between the Carlsons' and Greenes' houses was a crowded place. All the Youngs, all the Blakes, Carlsons, and Greenes were sorting out camping gear and cramming it all into John's brand new Escalade. The parents were still trying to figure out a way to call all this to a halt, and yet seemed glad all the excitement and planning of the last six months had come to an end.

After all was packed, goodbyes said, and hugs from moms, the ship was ready to sail. Chris won the coin toss between him and Jason to see who would start driving. Tim, coming from a lifetime of being around new cars, could not care less. With a grin that pushed his ears far back on his head, Chris rolled the good ship down the driveway, waving like the British Royals.

Eight hours later with Illinois and Wisconsin behind them in the dust, the voyagers entered Minnesota at Duluth. As they continued north up the North Shore Drive in Minnesota, Tim said, "This is the most awesome road I've ever seen. Look at that ocean."

Oh, oh, there's a bad memory, Jason thought. *I called it an ocean one time myself. Keep your lips locked, Jason. Let someone else tell him it's not an ocean.*

"Actually, Tim," said Mr. Carlson, "think of your geography. An ocean in Minnesota?"

"Oh no, I don't believe I said that. It's Lake Superior isn't it? Looks like an ocean though, doesn't it? Let's not let this get back home, huh, guys?"

With a final stop at Tofte, Minnesota, for gas, junk food, potty, and directions, John Carlson drove the final twenty-four miles on dirt road to the outfitters.

Again Tim was taken by the sight. "Our family has traveled a lot around the country and even beyond, but I've never seen so many trees. All so high and tight together - and so green; so many shades of green. I thought there would be lakes around here."

"There are lakes, lots of them," Jason said. "When we get to the outfitters, all you'll see is lakes and trees. Boy, we sure sound like a bunch of hicks on a lost planet."

"Well, coming from our cornfield, what do you expect?" Chris said.

Upon arriving at the outfitters after the twelve hour ride, they unwrapped their bones out of the car they now called their "Space capsule."

"What's that smell?" Tim asked.

Jason again could not contain his tour guide urge. "That, my friend, is the scent of pines, fresh air, and clean water. Look how blue that water is. Not like the brown lakes and rivers in Illinois. Get used to it. It's our new home for a week – and remember it always."

After registering their presence at the desk in the outfitters, the little troupe quickly set up camp for the night.

Jason woke up early the next morning with the sound of birds and the smell of smoke from nearby campers having breakfast. "I was so tired last night I don't remember bringing my second leg into the sleeping bag," he said loudly, so the others would wake. "What's for breakfast? I'm hungry."

After a lumberjack breakfast in the lodge, the owner of the outfitters pulled John aside into another room as the guys picked up their prepackaged food packs and loaded them and the gear they brought with them, into Moose's new orange pickup.

"Still driving an orange truck, Moose?" Jason said.

"They still shoot guns around here in the fall."

"Hey, Mr. C., what did the owner show you in that room," Chris asked.

"I'll tell you at the end of the trip, if you remind me."

It was a short drive down to the landing where two aluminum canoes were waiting. Loading the canoes and wrapping all the gear under plastic, Jason relived these special minutes of memories when all this was new to him. Now it was Tim's turn to ask the dumb questions.

"We gonna get all this stuff in just *two* canoes? Who's gonna do the steering? Why the plastic over the stuff? How long is it gonna take to get to the end of this lake?"

Moose grinned at Jason. "I still remember you asking the same questions five years ago."

"With all the people coming and going here, you re-member me and dad?"

"Sure do. I remember the special ones. I also remember how you started to paddle, got twisted around, and rammed the pier with the canoe all at the same time."

"Not funny, Moose ... Yeah it is. Let's just not tell them, okay?"

Chris Young and John Carlson got into one canoe with John in the stern, and Tim Blake and Jason in the other, with Tim in front. As they pushed away from the pier, Jason remembered his first sight from the front of the canoe five years ago and now he knew what Tim was seeing for his first time. Just the water, clear sky blue water and a gentle up and down motion of the canoe.

"Hey, this is great," Tim said.

"You'll get your turn back here. You'll love it," Jason warned him.

Sawbill Lake was a long narrow lake, and as the sailors settled into their efforts sometimes the two canoes would drift out of earshot of each other.

"How's it going so far, Tim? You're quiet. Still think you made the right choice in coming along?" Jason asked.

"Yeah, but I don't know if I should sit on the seat or kneel like I see Indians do."

"Try both ways and see which you like."

Tim slipped off the seat and put his knees on some rivets on the bottom of the canoe. "Ouch! That would be hard way to paddle for a long time."

Jason laughed to himself. *New kid on the trip. I'd put a sweatshirt or a jacket under my knees.* "I bet you decided to sit, huh?"

"You got that right."

They all began to dip paddles deeper into the water, take longer strokes, trading off paddling from one side to the other. The one in the rear would switch according to the guy in front when he wanted to change sides, usually for comfort reasons. But because the one in the stern does the steering, he had to adjust his strokes to keep going straight.

Jason and Tim suddenly realized they were being overtaken by a vessel off their port side doing twice their speed.

"So you want to race, huh?" Jason said. "Dig in, Tim. We can play their game too."

Tim tried his best to compete, but on his first canoe trip

from the cornfields of Illinois he couldn't coordinate the swinging of the paddle fast enough without banging it on the canoe. At one time he lost his grip and dropped the paddle in the water. Jason, also inexperienced in this fine art of canoe racing, had to turn the canoe around and go back to pick it up, loosing at least ten minutes of the race. During the recovery of the paddle, Jason and Tim heard Chris and John laughing as they put more and more distance between themselves and the losers.

After twenty minutes of their glorious victory, Chris and John looked exhausted, waiting for Jason and Tim to catch up.

The two canoes moved closer together as they approached the north end of Sawbill Lake, and the four voyagers got their first look at the portage adventure. They beached the canoes where the wooden sign read, *Ada Lake 78 Rods.*

"Rods? Whoever measures things in rods? How long is a rod?" Tim asked.

"You tell him, Jay," Chris said. Then he added, "You shocked the entire math class a few years ago with your answer."

"We're standing on the very same dirt I was when I learned it. A rod is sixteen and a half feet; that means the portage is abou…"

"I can do the math, Greene. That's about thirteen hundred feet. Hey, it's long."

"You figured it out that fast?"

"Math is one thing I'm good at," Tim answered.

When all the gear and packs were hung on their backs, and Jason with an added backpack on his chest, only the canoes were still on the ground. Tim was the one with the tenderfoot questions.

"Do we come back for the canoes?"

"No," Jason said, "the servants will bring them to us."

Tim actually looked around, until the others all broke out laughing.

"Two of us will have to add the canoes to our own load. Today that's you and me, Chris."

The extra beef Chris carried on his own frame, along with some wrestling experience, made him about the strongest one among them. Five years ago, on this very spot, at age twelve, Jason remembered how he struggled to lift the canoe, only to fail in his dad's sight. He promised his father he would lift it on their next trip, not knowing it would be five years later and without his favorite friend.

Now that the others were out of sight he took a minute to reflect on that trip. Then with two packs on his shoulders, an expanded chest, legs set apart, much more strength and determination, he leaned over and closed his large fists around the gunwales. In a massive muscular thrust he swung the seventeen foot, sixty-five pound canoe up over his head with the other backpacks. In a loud voice of victory he unashamedly yelled inside the aluminum cavity, "Dad, look! Dad, I did it!" He planted one foot ahead of the other and stomped up the trail leaving his size twelve boot prints in the face of mother earth.

Ahead of him he could hear John encouraging Tim to bear his load, and Chris banging his canoe into tree branches while using the Christian equivalent of swearing.

When the crowd assembled at the other end of the portage, now about noon, Tim was trading his shorts for a pair of jeans. "Okay, okay, I understand the mosquito thing. Don't bug me about it."

The word "bug" made all the others burst out laughing.

"No bugging here," Chris said.

"These jeans gotta last me all week. I only brought the one pair. Yeah, I know you told me to bring two, but I don't learn so easy. Hey, that was a portage, huh? See, I can handle it."

Lunch was devoured at the end of that first trek. The packaged lunch for Tuesday was peanut butter sandwiches, cheese sticks and Kool-Aid. Chris was honest enough to make it known that the lunch wasn't enough. "Protein, I understand, but not much bulk. I need bulk"

When they put everything back into the canoes, Chris pointed across the lake. "Not a very big lake. I 'spose we do another portage over there, huh?"

"Yep," Jason said. "But the map shows our campsite for tonight is in this lake."

"Let's hope it's not occupied," John Carlson said in a low voice.

"Whew," Tim said. "At least we can sleep before another portage."

Jason leaned close to Chris. "Don't tell him the worst one is coming tomorrow morning."

Only a half hour into Ada Lake and they spotted the campsite – vacant. It was just mid afternoon, but they all agreed this was enough canoeing for the "cornfield boys" today.

Setting up their little village took longer than they anticipated on this first day. In some places there was not enough ground to put a tent stake into, because rocks were everywhere. They set up the two tents, started a fire in the circle of rocks with fire wood from a nearby pile.

"Where did that firewood come from? Somebody's job to keep this place supplied with firewood?" Chris asked.

"Nope," Jason said. "Dad told me that it is the responsibility of all of us as we collect wood, to leave some for the next guy."

"That's pretty cool. It works," Tim said.

After supper that first day and dousing the fire, hanging the food packs from trees, the exhausted bunch crawled into the tents: Tim and Chris in one and John and Jason in the other.

In the quiet quarters of their small tent, Jason said, "I hope I don't show too much emotion tomorrow when we get to the place I named Frosty Point. The memories of Dad and me are so strong there. After his death, that canoe trip came to mean an awful lot to me. What we talked about and things he told me have become so real to me these past years. I hope I don't break down and make a fool of myself."

"If I were a dad, and had a son think of me like that, I'd consider myself a rich man," John said. "Don't worry about it, Jay. I'm sure the guys know how you feel and they'll respect you for it. If all else fails, I'll distract them somehow. Okay? Jason, do you hear me?"

Jason yawned. "Sorry, I was dropping off there. Thanks."

Chapter Thirty-Two

Throughout the night it rained and soaked the campsite and seeped into the tents. From Chris and Tim's tent some hard language unrolled with highly colorful descriptions of a wet sleeping bag.

"By the choice of those words I know that's not Chris waking up," Jason said.

When they all crawled out of their cocoons, they saw and smelled a very wet and dripping campsite with streaks of sun trying to break through the canopy of trees and the early morning mist. John dug out his camera.

Tim was the first to pose another problem. "Okay, in this wet and wild world we're standing in, how do we start a fire? Look at that pile of wood – it's soaked."

Jason and Chris were shaking their heads with the same hungering question. But Jason noticed that John had a grin on his face as he brought ten dry sticks from his tent.

"You slept with wood in your sleeping bag?" Jason said, laughing.

"You laugh now, but I'll get a fire going, won't I? I bet you think I'm going to share it with you, don't you? Think ahead, guys. We've got a week to go."

A breakfast of bacon and eggs, juice, coffee cake, and

coffee, never tasted so good. Not enough for the growing boys, but tasted good.

With John, Jason, and Chris being Christians they started this day off with some words of devotion and prayer. Tim questioned what was going on, but said he respected the others. "I thought that only went on in church."

"Being a Christian is a full time, everyday 24/7/365 thing," Chris said. "Besides, look at this place. It's one big church."

"Yeah, you could say that," Tim answered. "The streaks of sun coming through the trees look like those old Bible pictures I remember from Sunday school papers."

"You went to Sunday school, Tim?" Jason asked.

"Yea, back in the day, in another world when I was a little kid."

The three believers looked at each other with gratifying grins.

After stowing all the gear in the canoes again and making sure the fire was out, the flotilla paddled off to Frosty Point, with a couple of lakes and portages to conquer first. At the north end of Ada Lake, where the rapids were five years ago that led into Skoop Lake, they found a pile of logs packed together in hard dried mud.

Tim stood up in the bow of the canoe, pointing ahead like George Washington on the Delaware River. "What's that? How do we get over it?"

"Say hello to your first of many beaver dams. We get to the other side by sliding the canoes up, over it, and walking on it," Jason answered.

"Won't it cave in?"

"Not a chance. That thing is about as strong as your own house."

They pulled the loaded canoes up on it, slid them across

the dam and then into a thin swamp where the rapids were five years ago, and finally into the water of Skoop Lake in less than ten minutes.

In true Tim Blake fashion, he said, "And just where were the beavers?"

"They're probably watching us."

"That's spooky."

"Too bad all portages aren't that easy," Chris said.

Only twenty minutes on that lake and a sign, *180 rods to Cherokee Lake* smiled at them from the start of the next portage.

"This is it, Chris. The ugly one," Jason whispered.

They unloaded the gear, and Tim said, "Is this the one where I carry the canoe?

"Okay by me," Jason said. "Think you can handle it?"

"No problem. I'm as strong as you. Give me another pack too. It's my time to join the leaders on this trip."

Oh, how pride goes before a fall. He has no idea what he is about to step into, Jason thought.

At 180 rods, or over one half a mile, the portage became a challenge for all of them.

The rain that soaked their campsite at Ada Lake had visited this portage as well. Wet paths, slippery rocks and roots, wet and low hanging branches, and steep hills both up and down, tested the souls of all.

Going down one steep hill, the rear of the canoe Tim was carrying banged on the rocky path behind him. The rope tied to the bow of the canoe had come loose and was hanging down in front. He stepped on it many times, hurting his shoulders by jerking the front of the canoe down and drawing highly crafted words from his lips.

The little parade had spread out according to the strides and slips of each man. The unending flow of Tim's vocabulary identified where he was in the lineup. Especially after he slipped on a slimy root and slid, back side down, thirty feet to the bottom of a ravine, still attached to his two back packs and one sixty-five pound canoe. When Tim recovered at the end of the slide he was so mad, even his terminology failed him. Jason guessed that Tim's brain was suddenly calculating the sanity of joining this epic expedition.

When the group finally assembled at the end of the ordeal, the three Christians wondered what they would hear from their lost sheep. Within a few minutes they heard, from under an approaching upside-down canoe, "And I asked to come on this pilgrimage and abuse myself, didn't I? Now I have to spend the rest of the week in these cold, wet, and muddy jeans. Ask me if I'm having fun yet."

No one asked.

After a well deserved rest, all the provisions were loaded again into the little ships. They had to paddle through another narrow swamp before breaking out into a sight that demanded cameras. All four of them whipped out their digitals from their waterproof holders and took pictures of the south end of Cherokee Lake. An absolute perfect calendar picture of glassy sky blue water reflecting fluffy white clouds with a smattering of small tree covered islands. One of the islands was all bare rocks, except for just one spindly tree standing on the middle of it.

"Now that's the coolest island I've ever seen," Tim said. "I'll bet that tree gets lonely."

"Lonely? Blake, trees don't get lonely," Chris added.

The still water was surrounded by tall grass and pine trees that seemed to keep reaching to the sky.

Birch, ash, and oak trees added their color to the awesome scene. The four just sat and drifted while soaking the panorama into their cameras and retinas. Clean, crisp lung-cleansing air added another dimension to the experience. John obviously couldn't contain himself, and he prayed aloud.

"Now *that's* something to pray about," Tim said.

Cherokee Lake was larger than the others they had traveled on so far, and seemed more beautiful with each dip of the paddle. The lake was not only beautiful to the eyes, but refreshing to the thirst.

Chris said, "Moose told me the water is clean enough to drink from the center of the larger lakes."

"Chris, you gotta be kidding," Tim said. "Fish dump in the water, you know."

"He's right, Tim. You *can* drink it. We learned that when Dad and I were here the first time," Jason said. "That's what these water jugs are for. The center of the big lakes is where we get all the water for drinking, cooking, and cleaning dishes."

Tim shook his head. "I still think there's something I don't like about the idea."

No choice, no option, no other way, echoed in Jason's mind from the first trip.

There was no rush to get through the lake. Time seemed to stand still and it didn't matter. Jason knew that the scene had captured the three restless teenage hearts, showing them there was a lot more to life than computers, Blackberries, cell phones, Facebook, twitter, and video games.

He twisted around to John. "I wonder what all this looks like in winter. It must be awesome."

"If you want to know that, you'll have to find someone else to come up here with you. Winter in this place is where I'd say No."

To himself, Jason thought, *I'm going to do just that.*

With who, I don't know yet, but I promise myself I will see this place in the winter some day. He turned around and sunk his paddle deep into the water.

Even Cherokee Lake had to come to an end, but Jason could see that a pleasant surprise waited for them at the north end. The portage to the next lake was so short they could glimpse the new water through the trees. With two of them on each side of a canoe, and space to walk, they carried one, and then the other canoe the fifteen rods to Gordon Lake, which was long and narrow.

When they all sat to rest, John walked into the shelter of the trees and Tim turned to Chris. "Mr. C. is a religious kind of guy isn't he?"

"He's a Christian like Jason and me." He grinned at Jason. "That makes us religious too?"

"I never thought of you guys being religious, but you all fit the same mold."

"Does being 'religious' make you think different about us?"

"No, but he prays as if he knows God like a friend."

Chris nodded. "He does. I'm glad you see that. *We* know God like a friend too. That's what being a Christian is all about – a relationship with Christ. Did you notice how the beauty of the last lake just pulled a prayer out of Mr. C.?"

"Yeah, I can understand that now. This is a rough place, but I can see what God did here."

"You can? You think God did all this?"

"Isn't that what *you* would say?"

"Sure, but it's good to hear you say it." Chris turned to Jason with a look of understanding, and Jason sat for a while thanking God that Tim was seeing Christ in him and the others.

Suddenly breaking off the conversation, Tim pointed

and yelled. "Hey look! Two moose, or is it mooses or moosi? They're looking right at us. They can't be fifty feet away."

"What's all that stuff hanging off their horns and out of their mouths?" Jason asked.

Tim shot back quickly. "That stuff, that you call it, is swamp weed. And those aren't horns, they're antlers."

"Antlers, horns; what's the difference?"

Tim gave an exaggerated sigh. "Biology, Greene, Biology. You sleeping in class? Horns are permanent and don't usually branch out or stop growing. Antlers are shed each year."

Looking at Tim with a tilted head and wide eyes, Jason said, "Hey, nice going, Blake. Now look who has all the wildlife answers. Horns, antlers, still the same to me. I know God did His best to make all the animals, but with all due respect to our friends over there, He sure was scarce with handsome when He made the moose."

Cameras started clicking again and Jason zoomed his lens to telephoto to get a close-up of one of the faces, hanging weeds and all.

At the end of Gordon Lake, another on-the-trail lunch of summer sausage and cheese sandwiches, fruit jerky and Kool-Aid quickly disappeared while they looked at another sign, *Frost Lake 160 rods.*

Tim was first with a comment. "You guys going to pray about this one before we start? If it's anything like the last portage, I'm going to have to ask God what He had in mind when He put this part of creation together."

Jason, John, and Chris looked at each other, and Jason knew they were all thinking the same thing: *He's catching on.* Jason noticed that John was taking advantage of Tim's question, and he closed his eyes as though praying for the coming trek. Jason guessed from Tim's expression that he was thinking, "*I didn't think he was really going to pray, just because I said so!*"

The 160 rod portage or 2,640 foot stroll wasn't so bad. In fact, a cakewalk compared to that 180 rod beast they had fought earlier that morning. Another small lake, another beaver dam and after thirty minutes the fleet rounded a bend and there, in all its empty glory – Frosty Point, named by twelve-year-old Jason himself after the cold nights he and his dad spent on that spot five years ago.

Off to the right of the campsite lay a 500 foot sweeping pure sandy beach inviting them all to jump in for a swim. That is, if anyone felt they could stand the liquid ice. After testing it with a foot from Chris, they stayed on land.

Again it was mid afternoon and camp was set up faster now that they were experienced. Together they decided they would spend the entire day there tomorrow and plan what to do after that.

When the pots were washed after a spaghetti dinner and the fire stoked for conversation, the four friends sat on stumps. The talk went from nothing to nowhere as casual talk usually does. Then out of the blue, Tim threw the gauntlet down again with, "Is there really a hell?"

"How'd you answer that, Mr. C.?" Chris asked.

"I don't want to thump Bible talk on you guys, but answer this first. Is there a heaven?"

"Sure, we all know that," the boys answered.

"What do you think heaven is like?"

Jason answered, "A nice place, good people, being with God – all for ever."

The others nodded their heads in agreement.

"Right," John said. "It's comfortable, joyful, bright, fun and fellowship with loved ones and an everyday banquet for you, Chris. Well, just as there is a heaven, there is a hell.'

"There really is?" Tim said. "I always thought it was just a joke for us defective guys."

"You're not defective, Tim. What have you heard about the hell side of things?" John kept the questions coming.

"Well, it's bad, wrong, fire, and hot stuff. Tough and mean like that long nasty portage we did this morning – oh yeah, a lot of friends there too."

"Don't count on friends being there. It *is* a nasty, fearsome, torturous, miserable, dark, putrid and very lonely place. Tim, if you want to really understand the ugliness of hell, research it out in the Bible and some books I can recommend to you. In simplest form, there are only two places we enter after death: heaven or hell. That's too simple for some to accept, and too simple for 'educated' minds to comprehend."

"Sounds terrible," Chris said.

"It's not a place to look forward to like a lot of people think it is – certainly nothing to joke about. There is only one thing heaven and hell have in common: it's for ever. No chance to change your mind. What makes this topic unique is that eternity is for ever, but you make the decision where you will spend it."

"A guy can choose to go to hell?" Tim asked

"You choose to go to heaven. Hell is the loser's option."

Jason nodded to Chris, and they left the conversation to bring the canoes higher up into the campsite and hang the food packs in the trees.

"How do you choose heaven, Mr. C.?" Tim kept the conversation going, just loud enough for Jason to hear.

"By accepting Christ as your personal Savior, Tim. Chris, Jason, and I have done just that. Watch them closely this week. Watch how they put up with the problems, obstacles, and setbacks that come up before this trip is over. Listen to their talk."

"Yeah, I never hear them swear like I do. How come?"

"Here they come. Just watch and listen. This conversation is just between you and me, Tim."

"I hear ya."

Jason carried on as though he had heard nothing, but he prayed silently that the Lord would open Tim's eyes to the truth.

Chapter Thirty-Three

The following day, Thursday, was supposed to be a sleep-in-late day, but chirping birds and the call of the loons on the lake seemed to have other ideas for the campers. John was up early, as usual, and the aroma of the bacon and pancakes was too much for youthful sleeping noses – especially Chris.

That morning heavy memories bore down on Jason, but he had prepared himself months ago not to get buried under them. Tim quietly asked him a question that snapped any old memories out of his mind.

"I never thought about this until just now, Jay, but I gotta go to the bathroom."

"Just do it like you've done it for the past three days - water the trees."

"I gotta do more than just water a tree."

"Oh, just take this roll of T.P. and do it in the woods – like a bear."

"I'm not a bear. Now tell me, how do you do it?"

"See that log over there? Sit on it, hang over and let nature be your guide."

Without moving a facial muscle, "You gotta be kidding - you *have* to be kidding."

"No choice, no option, no other way. Hey, if you find a

better way, let us know."

Tim tilted his head and frowned at Jason, grabbed the T.P. and stomped off into the woods with some more of his unique vocabulary.

After breakfast, Tim washed out his clothes that got muddy from the fall back on the miserable portage, and spread them out on a large rock to dry in the sun. Skinny dipping for the first time in their lives, the boys forced themselves to splash around in the water that was just two degrees above ice.

In full dress swimming suit, having put a toe in the water, John said it was definitely not for him. "Sorry, guys, it's too cold for this old boy. Besides, swimming this early in the morning in these lakes is not the smart thing to do. Did you ever realize it might be a tad bit warmer in the afternoon?"

Later in the morning the boys took turns soloing in the canoes and getting them out into the lake. Together they tried to swamp a canoe or sink it, but new ship technology prevailed and they stayed afloat.

About 1000 feet from land they could see a rock that looked about the size of a large bus. Jason paddled out to it and climbed to the top. Without anything to tie the canoe to, he soon discovered it was floating away and he had no way to get it. He yelled to the others at the campsite, but against the wind it was no use. The three on shore could surely see his dilemma, but pretended to ignore him for a long time, infuriating Jason. He caught on to their game and just sat down to wait them out.

After a few minutes he could see Chris and Tim having what looked like an excited conversation, pointing first at the drifting canoe and then at the rock. He tried to imagine how their conversation might be going.

"Ya know, Chris," Tim was probably saying, "if we don't go and get that canoe now, we'll have to paddle all the way across the lake and get if for him later."

And Chris was maybe replying with a shrug, "I 'spose you're right. He can't do anything. It will only be harder on us the longer we make him wait."

"Yeah, I think he knows that too. Let's go"

Yes, there they were, getting into their canoe, making a move at last!

Later, with a little chill among the friends, lunch was served after the rescue, soothing over the wounds. The sun was doing a good job drying clothes and sleeping bags they had spread over the rocks.

John carved a lounge chair in the sand and wiggled into a real nap. Tim suggested the three of them take a hike up one of the paths that went out from the campsite.

"You guys go on. I'll stay here," Jason said, sitting down by himself.

The two caught on to what Jason was thinking by the tone in his voice, and went on without him.

Now alone with only his thoughts, Jason really let his emotions carry him away. He thought deeply of the conversations he and his dad had on this very spot. *I'll bet these are the same stumps we sat on.* He thought of the time his dad tossed him over his shoulder like a sack of grain, the news of how he was conceived, the promises he had made to his dad, and had even broken since, as well as remembering his dad's advice on how to deal with some of the hard times and defeats in life. *"No choice, no option, no other way."* He was so thankful for those words. He'd used them often in the years since that trip.

Jason freely let himself slip back into a kinship with his

dad. *Dad, I miss you so much. Life sure isn't fair. I don't like going it alone without you. If you can watch me, I hope I'm doing things right. Now I see I did make some hard promises to you, didn't I? You tried to warn me didn't you? I wish you were here on this trip. We all miss you around town. Now that I'm a Christian, I know I'll be with you again sometime.*

With Tim and Chris gone, and John sleeping on the beach, he let himself go and had a good cry; even at age seventeen.

Later in the afternoon, after Jason had cleared his head, Tim and Chris returned from their hike and all three laid down for naps of their own in the warmer weather. After laying there for about a half hour with his hands behind his head, Tim stirred with something crawling on his chest. Jason noticed it and wanting to remain silent, tossed a stick to Chris, bounding it off his face, and waking him up. Before he could yell, he saw it too. A fat chipmunk walking up the front of Tim's sweatshirt, eating cookie crumbs on the way to Tim's chin.

Tim looked as though he couldn't believe what was going on. He just lay still soaking in the unforgettable event; without saying anything this time. In the meantime, John woke up, saw what was keeping the boys quiet and was able to get a picture. The snapping of the camera scared the bushy tailed critter away. Tim just laid there as though in shock, as if wondering if what he saw really did happen.

In the early evening they got out the maps and discussed the rest of the trip. They sat on logs and stumps, and surveyed the waterproof maps. Looking at the area, they noticed a huge lake called Brule Lake that was not too far from them. They decided to go through Brule Lake on the way back instead of returning the way they came.

"Look at this. Going through Brule Lake we'll have to navigate the Vern River to get back to the outfitters," John pointed out. "From what some friends told me a few years ago, the Vern River is not a friend to man, beast, or canoe."

"But look," Tim said, "it shows a solid line with many tiny lakes or ponds all in a row. We can coast down a river."

"Yeah, and it's only about two miles long," Chris said.

"I know I'm an old man in your sight and you think I'm looking for an easier way out, but if you go this way you're choosing a gutsy long and hard way back. Think about it, guys," John said.

The boys put their heads together in a huddle, talked over the pros and cons of the risks, and with the invincible confidence of teenage minds, put their hands together in a pledge of solidarity.

"We can do it. We can do it!" Tim said for all of them, with a valiant smile.

"Yeah, yeah, we're gonna do it," Jason added. "We're gonna push ourselves hard and prove to the world we're here. Chris, what's your word on this?"

"I'm in. We should do it."

With a grin, John said. "Okay, you guys, I'll let you find out. If you boys want to become men in the next two days, it's okay with me. I'm in it for the long haul."

Jason took a step back. *That's just something Dad would say, I wonder what he meant, 'become men in the next two days?' I'm in for trouble again I think. Dad would love this.*

All too fast a supper of chicken à la king, wild rice soup, fudge brownies and Kool-Aid slid down gullets. Still not enough, but by now they were used to not filling up. They cleaned up the pots and pans and Tim said he was glad to get back into his jeans that were now cleaned and warm. With the fire warming their chests, Jason was only vaguely aware that the temperature was sliding down with the setting sun.

"Why do you Christians think *everyone* should be a Christian?" Tim asked suddenly.

Jason was surprised but pleased at the way Tim always seemed to swing camp fire talk around to spiritual things. "Not just *us* that think that," he said. "Christ Himself said so when He told Nicodemus 'You must be born again.' The story is in the Gospel of John."

"Let me read it to him," Chris said.

He borrowed John's little New Testament and read about Jesus talking to Nicodemus late that night.

"That Nick guy, or whatever his name was, had a dumb question. 'Can a guy go back into his mother's womb?'" Tim said with a laugh. But he sounded genuinely interested and wasn't mocking.

Jason smiled. "The point is, Tim, we were born once physically, and what Jesus is saying here is that we have to have a spiritual birth as well if we want to enter heaven and avoid that hell we talked about last night."

"Why don't more people know this?"

Chris stood up. "That's a *good* question. How 'bout that, Mr. C.?"

"This might hit too close to home for one of you. It's because they don't go to church, or don't hear about it in the church they do go to, or just don't *want* to hear about it. Some people think spiritual things are too complicated, but they really aren't. A personal relationship with Jesus is as real as a friendship between you and me. We know each other, talk to each other, and care for each other."

"You talk to Jesus?" Tim shot back.

"That's what we do when we pray," John said.

"Wow, all you guys know Jesus like that?"

"Yeah, we do," Jason answered.

"Guys," John interrupted, "believe me, I don't want to break up this conversation, but we've got to get some sleep. You've chosen a hard trip for tomorrow."

When they got up and lost the warmth of the fire, Jason realized the bottom had fallen out of the nice warm day they knew. Temperature was now in the low 50s, and still sliding.

"We gonna get any sleep in this cold?" Tim asked.

With teeth chattering, Jason said, "I've been here before when it was this cold" *I won't tell you what Dad and I did, though!* "One of the tents is larger than the other. We could all crowd into it."

"Crowd is right," Tim said. "I don't think I like the sound of that. This is terrible. It's June and it's *this* cold? That bathroom log is a long way back there in the dark woods. I'm not cut out for this life."

"You're not cut out for the next two days either," John added, as though to himself, but loudly enough for Jason to hear, and the two of them exchanged a knowing grin.

Chris agreed with Tim, but after thinking said, "If it's warmth we're looking for, all in one tent is where we'll find it. How we going to do it, Mr. C.?"

"I'll be in the smaller tent with my down sleeping bag. It will work fine."

"Three of us sleeping this close together is one part of the trip we *don't* talk about – to *anyone*." With his personal punctuation, Tim made sure he was understood.

John winked at Jason. A few minutes later Jason whispered to John, "What was that wink all about? Dad tell you about our cold night?"

"Sure did, Jay. Like the happiest man on earth."

"Oh, Mr. C., just the thought of that memory makes me want to fall apart. Why am I so weak when it comes to memories of him?"

"Because you two shared a special love between father and son. Be proud and thankful for it. Very few guys know that."

The three boys wiggled into their little house and after a half hour of teenage guy talk they fell sound asleep.

Chapter Thirty-Four

The relentless call of the loon and the chirping of the birds all around them pulled Jason out of his sleep again on Friday morning, to find the others in his tent were also just waking.

"This is our big day," Tim said, as they crawled out into the cold air. "Today Mr. C. says we become men."

Jason caught a look on John's face that said, *Oh, if you guys only knew.*

"Let's eat and get going," Chris added.

They ate another breakfast of French toast & syrup, dried fruit and coffee, before packing everything up, filling the canoes and dousing the fire – leaving some wood for the next guy.

Steering to the port as they left Frosty Point they re-peated their route over a beaver dam, a small lake, that 160 rod portage into Gordon Lake, and again to the north end of Cherokee Lake.

In the center of the lake the lead canoe bumped onto a submerged rock and came to a stop. No trees, island, ground, or anything. The canoe and its two sailors just sat marooned on the top of a rock less than a half inch below the surface. Within a few seconds the next canoe was stranded with them.

"Boy, this is something," Tim shouted. "Grounded in the middle of a lake. Not on ground either."

Jason stepped out of the canoe and found the rock big enough to walk around on.

"Hey, Jay, I've got an idea. Stay where you are," Chris said. "Tim, stay in your canoe and back away. Get the canoes off the rock and we'll take a picture of Jason. It will look like he's walking on the water!"

Sure enough, when he raised his arms it looked like Jason doing the Jesus thing: walking on the water in his jeans, P.H.H.S. sweatshirt, and Chicago Cubs cap. Chris and Tim took their turn doing the miracle. John declined the opportunity to be so pompous.

The rest of the day was full of travel and hard work. They paddled through six lakes and at least five portages totaling 413 rods, or about a mile and a quarter of hilly, dirty, muddy, rocky, and rooted paths. At the end of every portage, eight legs felt the pleasure of sitting in the canoe.

The constant scene of tall pines so thick on the shore made them all wonder if anyone had ever walked among them. Knowing they had a long day ahead of them, lunch again was taken on the run.

"Jay," Tim said looking over his shoulder, "do you get the feeling we're being watched?"

"Who by?"

"Not by who. We haven't seen any 'who' for three days. I mean by 'what'."

"What, what, what, who, what do you mean?" Jason persisted.

"I mean moose, bear, beaver, chipmunk, or ducks."

"Sometimes I do, and I wonder what they think of us

four in our shiny little boats."

"Maybe they think we're the dumb ones."

"Would they be so wrong?"

During the heat of the afternoon, shirts found their way tucked under the seats and Jason thought his dad would have been proud of his son who was just a skinny white ghost on that first trip, but now was deeply tanned and had developed the muscular broad shoulders and narrow waist he had once possessed.

By late afternoon, neglecting the surrounding beauty, they kept to their resolve to cover a great distance. After a lengthy portage around an awesome waterfall, John, Jason, and Chris were at the far end of the path at Brule Lake waiting for the rest of the gear and the second canoe to arrive on Tim's back.

After about fifteen minutes, John said, "Jay, you'd better go back and see what's holding him up."

"I'll go with you," Chris said.

"No, Chris, let him do this alone."

Jason headed back up the trail wondering what mystery waited for him this time. He found Tim sitting next to the canoe that rested on a broken tree.

"Hey, let's go, Tim, we're waiting for ya," Jason said in a loud voice.

"You can wait till you know what freezes over. As far as I'm concerned, I'm done."

"Done with what"

"This portage stuff. This whole blasted trip. I've met my waterloo – my breaking point – my wall. Don't you get it, Jason? I've been beaten. Done with all my labors. Done with this *stupid* getting nowhere, no break canoe trip."

Jason felt like laughing, but could see in Tim's defeated eyes that nothing was very funny from where he sat. He also thought the time had finally come where he'd have to show some leadership, and there was nothing funny about the way he would have to do that. "You've got to finish the job, Tim. We're still wait..."

"And I told you how long all of you are gonna wait."

Jason's back stiffened and his patience broke, and in a commanding voice, "Get under that canoe and take it to the end of the trail. No choice, no option, no other way. *Do it!*"

"Jay, I can't go on."

"You can't go back either. It would take four days to go backwards. *Now get up!*"

"Not like you to yell like that, Jay. What makes you the boss?"

"No one else here to do it, Blake. *Now move!*" Jason picked up the front end of the canoe with one arm and grabbed a handful of Tim's T-shirt with his other, put him under the canoe, then dropped it on his shoulders.

"Gee, what's got into you?"

"Sorry, Tim. Remember you were in on this decision for this extra mileage. Mr. C. tried to warn us, but we all said we were up to it. He more than hinted that there was a tough trip ahead of us before we saw that black Escalade again."

With tight jaws, and without swearing this time, Tim started to move. Jason leaned over and scooped up the pack Tim was caring and followed the inverted canoe up the path. *Boy, he must be mad, he's beyond swearing*, Jason thought.

About forty feet from the end of the trail where Chris and John had the other canoe packed and ready to go, Jason could see Tim faltering. His legs began to buckle and he was swaying from side to side. Jason slipped up under the canoe right behind Tim and lifted the burden from him.

Without comment and without missing a step, as the canoe was lifted, Tim kept walking straight ahead to the water's edge. He just stood there a while, then without speaking he helped load the canoe. With the second canoe loaded the two silent crews shoved off into the big choppy Brule Lake.

Brule Lake was huge, and the canoes dipped up and down like ships in rough ocean seas. Running against the wind made paddling now harder than any of the other lakes they had been on. Tim was still gnashing his teeth, but Jason was glad he was taking his anger out on the paddle by making it work relentlessly. He could see Tim's shoulders bulge and snap with each stroke.

Out into the big lake, Jason and John took the time to fill the water jugs in the center of the lake. About halfway up Brule Lake they beached the canoes. Jason could see that a 78 rod portage into the first of three skinny lakes would take them to the start of the Vern River.

Evening began to close in on them and they were still some distance from their appointed goal for the day: the start of the Vern River. From his first visit, Jason knew that evening time does a wonderful thing to small lakes by making them smooth as glass, and that night was no exception. As the two canoes slid thirty feet apart through the still waters of one of the smaller lakes, Chris noticed it first.

"Look at the other canoe. Looks like its own reflection on a mirror. You could take a picture, turn it upside down and wouldn't know the difference."

Cameras again were put to use. Tim said nothing, but looked at the scene for a long time.

I think he's coming back, Jason thought.

Finally in the last minutes of daylight they came to the west end of Vern Lake where the maps showed the mouth of the Vern River was supposed to be. The darkness prevented them from finding the river.

John could hold back no longer. "End of the day, end of the lake, no river and no campsite. What now, men?"

The following silence was so loud it hurt. Another fifteen minutes paddling in circles produced nothing worthy of a statement from any of the three.

Jason realized the only wisp of a solution was another big rock, about half the size of a house jutting up about six feet out of the water in the middle of the lake. They pulled the canoes all the way to the top and found no ground to pitch tents. They cleared a space of broken branches, small trees, and scrub large enough for four sleeping bags to be laid out on a thick bed of moss. With no plans or place for a fire, supper was as cold as the rock.

The single good thing they had going for them that night was a sky with broken clouds, bright moon and rather warm air. Tim was clearly still not having a good time, but appeared to be keeping his mouth shut, for the sake of all – himself included. Jason watched him stretch his angry mind and body on his sleeping bag, where he seemed to be reflecting on his meltdown that afternoon but was probably too embarrassed to say anything to the others, especially Jason.

Tim muttered in one decibel above silence, "I wonder what life-changing ordeal waits for me tomorrow."

Within what seemed to be just a few seconds, Jason realized that was Tim's final squeak and thought for the day. He had fallen asleep.

Chapter Thirty-Five

Morning dawned way too early – as usual. "Don't these birds and ducks have anything better to do? Here it is Saturday, don't they ever sleep in," Jason yelled, to start off the day.

"Saturday?" Chris almost yelled. "We're supposed to be home by tonight. I won't get to church tomorrow for the first time in years. Dad will have a fit."

Tim crossed his eyes and rolled them back into his shaking head.

"Easy, Chris, I clued him in before we left that we might be a day late in our return," John said.

Chris nodded. "Dad sure is a stickler about this church thing. I guess he's going to have to come unstuck tomor-row."

Because of enthusiastic eating habits earlier in the week, supplies in the food stores were dwindling. They searched the food packs and knew they needed something for lunch later in the day, just in case they were not at the outfitters by that time, but hoped they would be there by noon – supper, for sure.

Breakfast, in the meantime, again was pancakes looking more like scrambled eggs – and this time without syrup. The juice and coffee were gone, so they were glad Jason and John had remembered to fill the water jugs in Brule Lake the day before.

Chris muttered, "And we're 'sposed to survive on this for a whole *day*?"

After using some creative solutions to the modern plumbing culture, they lowered the canoes off the rock, loaded them again, and shoved off in search of the Vern River. Thanks to daylight and fresh bodies, they found it in five minutes.

"Here we go, guys. Take a deep breath," John said.

"Hey, Mr. C., you really do know something we don't, don't you?" Jason said.

John smiled and pointed ahead. For about ten minutes, canoeing on the little river was pleasant, but entering a swampy area they felt their world closing in on them. Soon they came to a small tree across the river that now was only a creek. A creek flowing in the direction they were going, but with no real advantage.

Tim, being in the front of the first canoe, grabbed the hatchet, taking out some leftover anger from the day before, he tossed each half to the sides. The fleet sailed single file while the sailors used the paddles to push themselves away from the high muddy banks. They soon came into a small pond about the size of the Dawg Hause parking lot.

Chris said, "That wasn't so bad. The maps show five more ponds like this, and the river between. I've got this figured out. We'll be done with this thing in about forty-five minutes to an hour. We'll be through the next few lakes and portages, showered up, and clean clothes on by three this afternoon. Dinner at a table with a tablecloth, cloth napkins, and candles in the lodge by five or six at the latest."

"Yeah, right. Tablecloths and candles," Tim mocked with

just moving lips and shaking head.

Shortly after they left the first pond, the river came to a standstill in a thick swamp. The canoes stopped completely in the shallow water. Jason was the first to realize that "someone" would have to get out of the canoe to lighten the load so it could be pulled or pushed for a while.

He rolled up his jeans and climbed over the side and slipped his feet into the cold water. Although he touched bottom quickly, he felt his feet, then ankles and then knees sink into the thick, gristly mud.

He was about to yell at Tim not to get in the water, but it was too late. Tim was into it up to his knees also. His face didn't look too good either. He just shook his head and pulled the canoe, *Must still be beyond swearing,* Jason thought.

"It feels like quicksand," Tim muttered, as though to himself. "Who would care anyway?"

Jason kept silent to match Tim's angry attitude

The occupants of the following canoe followed suit and for the next half hour all four played the part of Humphrey Bogart in *The African Queen.*

They came upon a large tree lying across the river and had to lift the canoes up and slide them over the tree, back into the muddy water. A sigh of relief and a small cheer, only by Chris, went up when they saw their next pond.

Pushing the canoes to a pile of rocks at the edge of the pond, they climbed out of the water yelling new-found words of terror. Their legs were full of ants, leaches, and other unnamed assorted crawling life. They brushed and picked the varmints off and checked each other for more, and swished their shoes in the water to get the parasites out of them.

"You knew it was this bad, Mr. C., and you still let us get

into this?" Jason asked.

"I couldn't help it, guys. You were so determined."

"We're like the early pilgrims wandering in the un-known," Jason reflected, with a sigh.

By this time the bulky, once bright orange, lifejackets were stowed deep into the pile of gear. They found them to be almost useless in this muck and mire. They were getting very dirty and were only another method of collecting bugs and whatever else might climb on. Besides, Jason guessed that their teenage egos thought it was cool to be bare chested in their struggles – more manly.

The pond was refreshing to say the least, but more of the glorious river lay ahead. Tim stripped to his boxers.

"What if someone sees you?" Chris yelled.

Tim snapped, broke his vow of silence, and in deep disgust, even where cussing failed again, barked out in a voice that silenced every swamp creature for miles around, "Young, *who*? *Who* see me? You see any signs of the human race around us in the last four days? Who else would be dumb enough to do the Vern River? This whole human experiment gives a new meaning to 'Where in the world are we?'" His venom showed no sign of letting up as he continued his rant. "We could all die right here, and no one would know where to look for our bodies in this mud. Any commonsense thinking search party would refuse to answer our call. You don't get it do you? We're – on – our – own."

An escape valve of tension was blown open, and Jason realized that in an instant, love for their expressive friend was warming three other hearts. John turned his head and had a good laugh. After a little thought, the other two boys got into the same uniform: old shoes, underwear, and a cap. John dignified his outfit with a swim suit.

"This is called a river on the map," Jason said, "but in

reality it's just a creek between five ponds. It's even getting narrower isn't it?" To move the canoes, all four had to take one of them at a time and pull it through the next part. John was on the port side at the stern and Tim was at the port bow. Jason and Chris were on the other side. With some hard tugging it moved slowly. Suddenly it floated freely, with Jason and Chris hanging onto their side.

Jason heard John in a quick prayer, "Dear Lord, come close."

When he looked over the canoe all he saw was Tim's cap floating in the water and John was missing too. After a long ten or fifteen seconds, John surfaced with a limp, gasping, and spitting teenage boy looking more like a soaked muskrat.

He put Tim's hands on the edge of the canoe, and said, "He must have stepped into a deep hole and sank fast. I couldn't see in the muck so I swung my arms and finally felt his flaying arms and I could pull him up."

Jason just watched Tim, not knowing what to expect from him after that.

Tim looked at John for a long time, then said, "Thank you, John. God bless you. I really thought it was all over for me. I've never been so scared in my life." Still spitting, "I got swamp up my nose."

By all four kicking their feet, the first canoe arrived in the next pond.

Looking back at the other canoe waiting its turn, John said, "Stay here, Tim, and rest. Now that we know what we're up against, the three of us can do it."

"What you're up against is that you need four on that job, John," Tim answered back.

Jason noticed that from that time on there was no more Mr. Carlson or Mr. C. It was John. Just John.

When all were safely in the next pond, Jason said, "I lost one of my shoes in the mud back there somewhere."

"Want me to go back and find it?" Tim said. "I've come to love this place in a very special way."

The other three looked at each other dumbfounded. No words fit the occasion.

"A joke, guys. A joke. You think I'd want to relive that thrill just for a shoe?"

From that time on, Jason went barefoot.

Just when they thought they had seen it all, in the next portion of the river they were stunned and sickened by the carcass of a big rat, the size of a dog, floating along beside their shoulders.

"It ain't a rat," Chris said. "It's a muskrat, and I think I see him smiling."

Tim was quick with his comeback. "He's got a good reason to smile. He's dead and doesn't have to live in this quagmire anymore!"

More bugs, gnats, ants, leeches, mosquitoes, beavers, and muddy banks with broken dead, stinking trees and floating carcasses now just became part of their normal day.

At about one in the afternoon they broke clear from the grip of the Vern River into Weird Lake. Jason imagined they could all hear the *Hallelujah Chorus* run through their minds. Except Tim, that is. But it was just his bizarre imagination, for which he blamed this ordeal.

Jason said, "Ya know, the name of the Vern River didn't sound so tough, but it sure beat us up. John, I think you knew what you were saying when you said we'd become men – we just did."

"I think that river we just came through should be called weird, not this lake," Tim said. "I'll bet there were a hundred species of wildlife watching our stupid parade in the past few hours, and they were all lying on their backs, laughing."

Chris said, "That five hours was the longest two mile trip I ever want to do."

They beached the canoes and got back into their dirty but dry clothes and hiking boots.

"Even these feel good," Tim said. "I want to thank you all for putting up with me these past days. John, or any of you, could have left me back there when you had a chance. No one would have known or cared."

Grasping Tim's hand, John said, "You're worth it, Tim."

Lunch was whatever was left over in the bags. Breakfast, lunch or dinner stuff – food was food – and now it was all gone. Every thought was on the hope of finishing this odyssey and being at the lodge for the next meal, tablecloths or not: heck, tables or not.

"It's a good thing we don't have mirrors with us," Jason said. "You guys look a fright – dirty, knotty, uncombed hair, sunburned skin, and beards."

"You don't look any better with that crazy one long eyebrow. You've got little weeds hanging from your face, like on that that moose we saw just the other day," Chris answered.

It seemed that only Tim could find something positive out of the situation. "We still have cameras. We can show the people back in the cornfields the day we became real men."

"The fragrance we've picked up isn't the greatest around here either," John said. "We must fit right in with the animals. We smell like them too. Good thing cameras won't bring that back."

Every mile they put between themselves and the Vern River was a blessing. The waters of Weird, Jack, Kelly, Burnt, and Smoke Lakes slipped beneath the canoes, and the five portages were traveled with ease. Jason was painfully aware that there were four tired, reeking bodies in crispy, stiff dirty clothes, plugging along. His and Chris' jeans were so crusty that the knees were torn out from the brittleness of the dirty and muddy denim. They all pushed along, with visions of rest and food dancing in their heads.

Chris and Tim carrying the first canoe and gear looked startled when they heard voices other than their own approaching them from Smoke Lake. They stopped and spoke to strange humanoids in clean, pressed clothes.

"Hey, how's it going?" one of the strangers asked. "Nice place here, isn't it?"

Still using his razor tongue, Tim had the perfect answer. "Look at us, just look at us, take a whiff, and ask us that again. I hope you have plans for the Vern River. You'll love it."

"The what? We're just going into the next lake and camp there for three days."

"Smart move," Tim said, as he leaned over and scooped up a near empty back pack and slung it over his shoulder.

The portage from Smoke Lake back to Sawbill Lake was a mere 102 rods, now just a summer stroll.

"I'm going to miss these walks in the park," Jason said.

Tim nodded with, "Yeah, like a root canal."

The lightened loads without food, and with the experience of the men in the canoes, made the paddling back to the outfitters a breeze.

Chapter Thirty-Six

Jason thought the sun looked as tired as they did, as it faded fast on the final day of the epic journey when they arrived back in civilization. The welcomed showers, fresh clean clothes from the stash in the car, and burgers in the little lodge store with low lit lamps, wood floors, chairs to sit in, and other people to talk to – it felt like discovering civilization and culture all over again.

Conversations went all over canoe country like fish stories; everyone outdoing the other with the biggest tale. But when the mention of doing the Vern River slipped out of Tim's mouth, the whole place went silent, jaws froze open, and all eyes fell on him.

A voice from ten feet away said, "The Vern River? The Vern River? Who said that? Who was ill-bred enough to do the Vern River?"

The four from the Prairie Heights cornfields looked at each other and said nothing, slipping down in their chairs, hoping no one would press the comment. John quickly and quietly slithered away from the table and out the door.

Jason knew that Moose had seen his face go beet red in an instant, and the bulky man obviously could not let a good chance like this get away. Pointing to Jason and his friends he said, "I'd bet it was them guys."

Out of a mix of anger and glorious victory, Tim stood up and defiantly waved his hands. "Yeah, it was us. What's so bad about the Vern River?"

Most of the outfitters' staff laughed. One of them said, "The Vern River is off limits to us. Four guys from Minneapolis tried it in 1966, and barely made it out alive. No one that we know of has had the guts to try it since."

Tim sat down, weak as a kitten and facial arteries throbbing a deeper red than Jason's. Hungry as they were, the remaining burger parts were left on the plates. Jason and friends didn't know whether to walk out or run out; proud or ashamed.

Dark had covered the campground two hours before, and Jason's weary bones were ready to be folded up into sleeping bags one last time. Suddenly Tim whispered in his ear, "Can we take a walk?"

John and Chris seemed glad to find their tents and go horizontal.

As they walked barefoot, Jason considered that he and his friends were men now because they had conquered the Vern River. Nearing the landing, Jason felt there was something Tim wanted to say to him in private. He was right.

"This has sure been a special week for me," Tim started. "Thanks for asking me to come with you. It must have been hard at times for you the way I acted and spoke, but I learned a lot from you guys. I always thought Christians were wimps and losers. When I saw what you guys put up with and how you never quit, like I did, you showed me real men can be Christians."

"We *are* real people. We've just accepted Christ as Lord of our lives and let Him guide us in what we do and say. We still have to go through the same swamps of life that everybody does. Pardon the analogy."

At the water's edge, Tim stopped Jason with an outstretched arm on his chest. "Look, Jay, the stars in the water." The still water after dark reflected a clean, bright starlit sky. "This is awesome. I've never seen anything like it in my life." Pointing to the sky, "What's that blurry area over there?"

"That's the Milky Way."

"The what?"

"The Milky way. We don't see that from a city because of all the lights. It's a bunch of stars; millions and millions of suns really, so far away they just look blurry. You sleeping in science this time?"

"This is incredible. I feel like I'm looking at God in the face. How can I get to be a Christian, Jay?"

Jason wished John was there with them. He could answer the questions better, but he knew he was on his own – with God's help. "Tim, it's a matter of believing in Christ and asking Him into your life as Lord."

"Sounds easy. How?"

"There are Bible verses and books to read that show the way, but it goes something like this. God loves you, has a great plan for your life, and wants you to know peace in your heart. Sin has separated us from God, and Jesus is the only bridge back to Him. You can cross that bridge with a simple prayer. If you're serious, Tim, repeat this prayer after me."

Tim nodded, and with their feet dangling in the cool still water, making ripples that spread out in circles turning the stars to sparkles, Jason started. "Dear Lord Jesus."

"Dear Lord Jesus."

"I know I'm a sinner and need Your forgiveness."

"I know I'm a sinner and need Your forgiveness."

"I know You died for my sins."

"I know You died because of my sins."

"I want to get rid of my sins."

"I want to get rid of my sins."

"I now invite You into my life and heart."

"I invite You into my life and heart."

"I want to trust You as my Savior and have You to be my Lord. Amen"

"I want You to be my Savior and Lord, and I trust You. Amen"

"Tim Blake, the angels in heaven are having a party right now for their new friend – you."

"You know, Jay, after the shower I felt clean, but now I feel cleaner yet. Is it always like this?"

"It can be. Keep in touch with God by reading His Word the Bible, hanging out with His people, Christians; and being a part of a Bible teaching church. To be honest, there are times we Christians get bumped around by sin and Satan. But Jesus has a great capacity for forgiveness."

Jason had an idea and thought about it to himself, then went on to say, "I don't know if it takes a real preacher to baptize someone, but I'm going to baptize you, right here and now. Get into the water."

The water was only waist deep as Jason took Tim by the wrists, and said, "Jesus, I hope this is okay with You. In the name of the Father, Son and Holy Spirit, I baptize Tim Blake for Your kingdom."

He laid Tim all the way back under the water.

"Tim, you'll understand all this sometime. Don't you think we should get some sleep? It's a long drive back to our cornfield tomorrow."

On the way back to the tents they realized they were soaked. They stopped at the car and dug out some more dry clothes; anybody's dry clothes.

Chris was sleeping deeply when Tim returned to his and Chris' tent. As Jason crawled into his and John's tent he was sure Tim wanted to wake Chris up and tell him, yet he also knew Tim had a little common sense and would wait till morning to tell Chris the good news.

When Jason was wiggling into his tent, John woke up and said, "Where did you and Tim find the energy for a walk? Everything okay? Why are you wearing my old pullover shirt?

"I'll tell you tomorrow. There's a new brother in Christ tonight. Tim asked me how to become a Christian and I showed him – just like you showed me."

John rose up on an elbow. "Nice going, Jay. That's the way the Kingdom grows, one man at a time. I'm proud of you. Let me say, son, that your dad would be proud too."

"John, I even baptized him in the lake. Am I allowed to do that?"

John ruffled up Jason's hair. "Ask Pastor Larsen when you get home. For now let me say, well done, son. If there was more room in this tent I'd high five ya."

Early the next morning Jason learned there is no sleeping late in a crowded campground, just like there was no sleeping late at a campsite out on the trail thanks to the birds and loons. This time is was the smells of people cooking, and the noises of packing, driving off, and laughing, with an occasional barking dog.

The Prairie Heights four quickly dressed in anything and anybody's dry clothes, making them look like a troupe of clowns. In their haste to leave, they struck their campsite and just plain threw all their stuff into the Escalade and pointed it south. Breakfast would have to wait until Duluth.

Just as they were pulling out of the parking lot, Moose ran up and called, "Thanks for coming. Come back again soon."

"We will," Tim shot back from the steering wheel. "I'll never forget this place. It will be with me forever." He grinned as he punched Jason on the shoulder.

While traveling the twenty-four miles of dirt road, Chris remembered John told him to ask about the little trip to the other room just before they set off into the water. "Hey, John, what was it that the owner of the outfitters told you just before we shoved off?"

"Oh that. He just told me that even if we got lost, they would know where we were. There's a computer chip mounted up under the bow of each canoe. It can be read by a G.P.S. system."

"Good thing you didn't tell us. I would have stopped for sure and waited for a ride home. Funny, someone must have been watching that little blip working its way down the Vern River," Tim said.

Chris followed with, "Yeah, I'll bet they had their fingers on 911 more than once."

The four enjoyed a deep hearty laugh; something missing from most of the trip.

The blacktop highway back down the North Shore Drive with its ocean-like views again was a refreshing sight. Tim shared with Chris and John the news of his new birth the night before, and for miles the four enjoyed sharing the exciting news.

Jason said the grumbling noise they heard as they entered Duluth was the alarm from their stomachs saying, "Enough talk, feed me." They noticed a large billboard, *Granny's Kitchen. All you can eat pancakes.*

"Look at those pancakes, so golden brown."

"They're all nice and round too."

"Stacked on top of each other. Not looking like the burnt and crusty scrambled eggs we're used to."

"That's our place. Right, guys?"

Chris opened the glove compartment to get a tissue as they entered the parking lot and discovered a form of technology they had all literally forgotten about. "Look! Our smart phones – I can't believe we actually forgot about these, all of us."

"I'm going to call home – after I eat," Tim said.

"Me too," Chris added.

Jason nodded agreement. "You guys go ahead, order me that 'all you can eat plate.' I'm going to call Sharon."

"Call Sharon?" Tim said quietly, as he elbowed Chris on their way into the restaurant.

Entering the restaurant, the other three found a table, ordered and talked and laughed about the trip; mostly that last day on the Vern River. The food came and still no Jason. John looked out the front window and saw him sitting on a small stone wall, bent over.

"I'd better see if he's okay."

Just as John got to Jason, he stood up and it was clear he was almost in shock. "Jay, what's wrong?"

"Let's go in. I'll tell you all at the same time."

Jason started to eat, but after a bite or two he quietly told the others that Travis Veldez was dead. "Sharon said he and some friends were drinking heavily and drove into the trees above that ravine at the sharp curve on highway 6 east of town. It was such a mess no one knows who was driving. They had to cut the car and human body parts out of the trees with chain saws. The town is really bummed out." Jason dropped his fork and lifted his drenched face biting his quivering lower lip. "It happened a day after we left. No one could reach us, and they're already buried."

Quietly, Tim said, "I know you guys considered asking him to come on the trip instead of me. If he was here, he'd be alive and maybe he would have been the one you led to Christ, Jay."

"Don't let all the 'what ifs' send you guys into guilt," John said. "Travis and his friends knew the risks and consequences of their drinking. A hard way to look at it, but it was their choice. I'm truly sorry for you guys. You've lost some friends. But remember this, your lives are too precious to sink into a bottle. What can you expect when mixing drinking and driving?"

Breakfast was finished, but not enjoyed like they intended it to be. Conversation was quiet for the next few hundred miles. Other phone calls repeated the same story.

Each of the four shared their own thoughts about the canoe trip. John said he'd found it refreshing to see young men deal with the problems they came up with. Chris said he saw it as an adventure and confirmed his courage, and the loss of ten pounds. For Jason it was both closure, and an opening into new confidence that he was going to make his way in life without his dad. Tim told them for him, it was a discovery that Christians were not wimps, and was glad he became one of them in that beautiful place.

After a fast food lunch that they enjoyed better than breakfast, the trip continued a little more normal. Entering Illinois, John and Tim were sacked out in the back seat and Chris and Jason were sharing the driving.

"Jay, I sure wish you would reconsider coming with me to Northwest College in St. Paul. That University you're headed for will be a tough place for you."

Jason took a deep breath. "Don't worry about me, Chris. I can handle whatever comes my way. I'm strong."

24597008R00142

Made in the USA
San Bernardino, CA
01 October 2015